MUTUAL STRANGERS

AND OTHER MISADVENTURES IN NANJING

GU QIAN

Translated by

Jack Hargreaves

SINOIST

Published by Sinoist Books (an imprint of ACA Publishing Ltd)
London - Beijing

info@alaincharlesasia.com ☏ +44 20 3289 3885
www.sinoistbooks.com

Published by Sinoist Books (an imprint of ACA Publishing Ltd)
in arrangement with Phoenix Literature & Art Publishing Ltd
via Two-headed Duck UK

Author: Gu Qian **Translator:** Jack Hargreaves **Editor:** David Lammie
Cover Art: A. Bodrenkova **Proofreader:** Professor Yan Yixun

 A catalogue record for *Mutual Strangers and Other Misadventures in Nanjing* is available from the National Bibliographic Service of the British Library.

Paperback ISBN: 978-1-83890-585-9
Hardback ISBN: 978-1-83890-586-6
eBook ISBN: 978-1-83890-587-3

NANJING CITY OF LITERATURE

unesco
Member of the Creative Cities Network

ARTS COUNCIL ENGLAND
Supported using public funding by ARTS COUNCIL ENGLAND

This book is published with financial support from the Nanjing Fund for Literature Translation.

Sinoist Books is honoured to be supported using public funding by Arts Council England.

Mutual Strangers

and Other Misadventures in Nanjing

Gu Qian

Translated by
Jack Hargreaves

Sinoist Books

Mutual Strangers

I met Huang Qian just the once, about seven or eight years ago. I was recently divorced and had all this free time, so I found myself back with the old crowd, most of them single themselves. Nothing had changed. It was the same guys, getting sloshed together, playing cards, talking about women. And the woman who got the most airtime was Huang Qian. She was a real chicken rib, apparently –hardly worth the effort but it would be a shame not to try a taste. It was clear from all their jabbering that a few of the guys had had their chance with this Huang Qian, but none of them had sealed the deal. That had me interested. What was she doing hanging around with this lot if she didn't plan on getting some?

"That girl doesn't know the birds from the bees," said Xiao Ke, not at all bitter.

"That's no girl. That's a man with tits," said Zhu Jun.

What had Huang Qian done to hurt him? Zhu Jun was on his second marriage already, with a sweetheart for a wife. But he still acted like his time to find the one was running out. He had it even worse than the rest of them.

"Chicken-bloody-rib," Liu Chao grumbled. The look on his face said he knew first-hand what waited down that path. He was the one who introduced Huang Qian to our friends. My impression of Liu Chao – it's changed since then, of course – had been that he was a stingy git when it came to women. He never brought a single one to meet his pals, it didn't matter if he had a thing with a girl or not. No prizes for guessing why: they could be snatched from him. Or, if there was no spark yet, he wanted to keep them in reserve in case one developed. Huang Qian was the only exception, which might explain a thing or two.

Lao Bu still had Liu Chao beat though, for joke of the group. To be fair to him, he had been divorced for years by then and hadn't once managed to bag himself a pretty lady to mend his broken heart, so his desperation was at least understandable. Lao Bu told us he had once taken Huang Qian back to his place and worked her the whole evening, only to get naked and not do the deed. "You got her clothes off at least, that's something," said one of the guys, envious.

"Yeah, right," said Lao Bu, looking back at him as if he couldn't believe his ears. "Who said it was her who stripped? She just sat there and watched me get my kit off."

We all creased with laughter. Then one friend, pointing at me, shouted over the noise, "Sounds like it's time we sent *him* in. See if he's still got it."

"He's got a point," the others chimed in. "Our man here survived a baptism by matrimony, and it's only added to his charm. He might get the job done."

"Yeah, let off a bit of steam for us."

"You show 'em. It's not a bad idea, that."

"What do you say?"

Thanks, was what I said, for them thinking so highly of me. I'd meet her if they were so sure. I wasn't all that interested, if I'm honest, but with everything they'd said about her, I had to.

The plan was to meet at Lao Bu's. And when the rest of us arrived early, our host could barely contain his excitement. He had done the cooking himself, and the table was filled with dishes. We were all settled in our seats, ready to dig in and getting impatient when Huang Qian finally sashayed through the door.

She was twenty-five and neither leggy nor much of a

looker. But I'll admit she had something. She was apple-cheeked with big eyes, and curvy with these perky breasts. The red check coat she wore hugged her in all the right places. I got the impression she might be a bit soft in the head, which suggested she was uncomplicated, and I struggled to tally what I saw with all the things my friends had said.

It had to be one of those, I guessed; she gave off that she was an easy catch, when the reality was the exact opposite. So how had she ended up looking for true love in a bunch of lechers?

The others introduced us, then we started dinner.

My friends had fixed it so that Huang Qian and I were sitting together, but beyond that, they left us to it. They barely said a word to either of us. Mostly they chatted among themselves, clearly to give us space to talk one-on-one. But they were disappointed. Once the meal started, instead of making any move, I stuffed my face and guzzled drink, remembering myself just enough to throw the odd scrap of conversation Huang Qian's way. This hacked them off, and they made it known. They shot me expectant looks, and when I didn't react, turned to cracking jokes at the expense of me and Huang Qian. Shit like how we must be head over heels for each other and too excited to speak, how we were just waiting for a chance to let the fire of our love burn bright, how they were so desperate to see those sparks. It was so unnecessary. The jibes annoyed Huang Qian something rotten, too, probably because they were so transparent, and she sat there with a face like thunder for the rest of the meal. The moment everyone was done eating, she stood up and excused herself, saying she wasn't feeling well. "I'll see you get home," I said.

Once we were in the taxi, I turned to her and said, "They're just kidding with you, don't be mad."

"I'm not mad," she said.

I had thought about trying to comfort her before we said goodbye, but now I wasn't sure how to start. I also wondered whether I ought to ask for a number or address, as a courtesy, but I quickly dropped the idea. I wasn't planning on marrying her and she wasn't one to sleep around, so why bother? We spent the rest of the taxi ride in silence, and when we pulled up somewhere along Daguang Road, she got out, and I told the driver to take me back. I did peer over my shoulder through the rear window once we were moving again, and to my surprise Huang Qian was standing in that same spot, watching the taxi pull away. Something about this warmed me to her.

But I never saw her again. I also stopped running with that crowd. This was about when I started writing, I'd say, and I was making writer friends. It had also occurred to me that in whatever little time we have on this earth, while I wouldn't go so far as to say there's a respectable way of spending it, to waste every day buzzing around like a drone hoping to get laid is beyond boring.

* * *

This summer, I got an invite to a modern art exhibition.

I'll be the first to admit that I'm no expert when it comes to modern art. I'm not all that interested in it, for one. It's just never clear to me what the artist is trying to express. What are they trying to say with it? I accept that it's a crazy world out there, but it's not so mad that there is a man sprouting breasts all over his body or skyscrapers floating in the clouds. Both were photographs too. Don't ask me how they were taken.

There was also this exquisite little black case placed on a bench with a red velvet cushion inside, and on top was a single unravelled condom. What's that even supposed to mean? Did it symbolise the shackling of human desire? That our instincts need packaging? Well, why not just say that? Why go to all the trouble when you could just write whatever it is down on paper and stick it to a wall? That would work just as well. Or was I missing the beauty? I took a lap and cast an eye over all the weird shit on display. Dotted around there really were clusters of people paused in front of certain pieces seeming to try and take them in, appreciate them. What have you seen that I haven't you pretentious moron, I remember thinking. I'm not saying there weren't a few pieces that warranted some attention, it was just those were the ones no one wanted to be spotted ogling. One was a photo in the corner, blown up huge in black and white, of a pregnant woman, naked, with her humongous bump drooping down. I couldn't really say what the rest of her looked like, but that belly, I could hardly believe how big it was, and painted all the way around with calligraphy. Staring at it, I could feel my line of sight creep downward. If I'm being straight, that was the only interesting thing in the exhibition.

After my third or fourth pass of the knocked-up nude, I made my way to the exit. By the main door there was a long table where earlier a young woman had been sitting with a large visitors' book and a pen ready for anyone who came in. She wasn't there any more, and nor were the guest book and pen. In their place were some of my friends dangling their legs off the table, mid-conversation. I walked up to Yang Yuegong and asked what time we were eating.

"Be patient," he said. "Soon."

Yang Yuegong was the reason I was there. He was friends with one of the artists who had asked him to bring along any writer types for opening day. So there we were. But for me, showing support for a friend of a friend came second to getting a decent meal. Yang had promised us beforehand that when we were done at the exhibition, the organiser would take us all for grub at the Sheraton. But why when it was coming up six had nobody made any moves to go yet? I was starting to doubt if we would be fed at all.

"The artists are holding a discussion somewhere in here first," Yang explained. "When that's finished, we'll go for food."

So there was nothing for it but to patiently wait. I hopped up onto the table edge alongside my friends and listened to their chatting. Performance art was the topic. Lao Xu was telling the rest about some guy in Taiwan – incredible, he said he was – who for a whole year, under supervision, punched a timecard on the hour every hour, day and night. And the guy who for three years straight refused to enter a single room, under any circumstances. Well, fuck, I thought at the time, if those two aren't madmen they're saints. Wang Qi jumped in then, saying there had been an American artist who severed his little guy in front of an audience, probably having injected analgesic first. He chopped it into pieces like it was a sausage. Then he added, as if we didn't already feel the implied repercussions of this in our groins, "We only get one of these our whole lives." Woof, that's what's called an impactful performance. It also reminded me of something. "Did you see in the papers?" I said. "That story about the American lieutenant general who was sexually harassed."

A major had barged into her office and started pinching her nipples and grabbing her arse while she was in full military attire. He kept going until she was crying like a pig set for slaughter. Luckily her subordinates heard and ran in, or else the old maid might have struggled to preserve her virtue. It was an interesting story, I said, a different kind of performance art.

"How is that performance art?" asked Luo Jie.

"If that's not, then what *is*? Enlighten me," I replied.

This started a debate about how to define performance art. One of them argued that it should imitate natural processes, and its meaning lies outside the event itself. Another that performance art should be appreciable, full stop. Then someone suggested it was any behaviour undertaken with an envisaged result. I couldn't see how any of these theories disqualified the whole sexual harassment situation from being performance art; it had significance beyond the fact of the matter, the "appreciability" was undeniable and, as for the intent and result, they went without saying. I had a go at offering my own argument based on all this.

"What's important in performance art isn't the act," I said, "it's who is watching. If a person has an eye for art, then anything they look at could be art."

"What's the point in artists, then?" My little theory had irked Luo Jie.

But I didn't know what artists are for, I said, only that he ought to believe me when I said I wouldn't mourn their disappearance.

As we were going back and forth, a bald man about our age with a paunch and a slick suit walked in. I recognised him straight away. "Hey. Lao Bu," I called.

He started and spun around. Then a smile crept across his greasy face. "It's you."

I slid off the table and took him aside to a nearby corner. "You here for the exhibition?"

"Exhibition, my arse," he said. "I heard there was one, that's about it. But I'm here to see if there are any easy women about. This is where all the artsy teases are."

He peered over his shoulder and scanned the hall. "None here, though."

"You haven't changed one bit."

"It's like the search for truth, for me," he sniggered.

I asked after the old gang.

"Xiao Ke is married now, he never comes out any more. Zhu Jun is a bigshot CEO. His company's doing well, and he even has a sweet little thing on the side. His old lady gave him hell when she found out. Liu Chao was arrested not long ago. The police found his number in some prostitute's contacts. I didn't think the fella had it in him..."

"And what about Huang Qian, how's she?" I didn't know where that question came from.

"You still remember her, eh?"

I nodded.

"That girl is one unlucky sod."

"Why?"

"This was last year. She found a lonely-hearts ad in some Hong Kong newspaper and wrote to the guy. He must have liked what she said because he wrote back and suggested a date in Shenzhen. He even sent a thousand Hong Kong dollars. But she was sick the day the letter came, off work for two days, and someone got a hold of it and opened it. They took the money and even plastered the thing up on the university bulletin board. She's part of the Youth League committee there. Apparently, when she went back and heard about what had happened, she turned sheet white and fainted. She had to be rushed off to hospital. They never got to the bottom of who opened the letter, not the school or the police. It was just left at that."

"How's she been since?"

"It really knocked her. She was sectioned. She's still at the hospital now."

"Shit," I said, probably too loudly. "You never think

that kind of thing really happens, but there you go. Frightening stuff."

Everyone in the hall had turned to look. "Scream it, why don't you?" Lao Bu didn't seem to like the attention.

* * *

We stumbled out of the Sheraton later that evening, pissed as farts. "Karaoke!" Yang Yuegong shouted. "Kara-oke! My treat."

Slurred cheers passed around the group. I said I was too tired, I'd pass.

"What's up with you? Something on your mind?" asked Luo Jie.

"Nothing," I said. "I've got to get some sleep. You have fun, I'll see you later."

My friends left in a taxi. I stood alone outside the hotel until I felt ready to take the busy street home. I was thinking about Huang Qian. I tried to picture the scene when she arrived at the psychiatric hospital, and the one years before of her standing on the street corner watching the taxi I was leaving in. Then I thought about my own life, about the years I'd been alone. It wasn't a good thought.

Everyone Has Their Song

The evening my brother-in-law arrived from Guangzhou, I bought a decent bottle of spirits and told the wife to put some grub on for us, and the in-law and I sat down and waited to get to work on them.

I liked this in-law, but not because he's my wife's younger brother or because he's short like I am. It was on account of his singing voice.

Anyone who has heard him will vouch that it's a good one. I was already a fan and I had only heard him sing the once before. He said himself that he was one of the Vienna Group's best singers, and he had a loyal fanbase at every teahouse he performed at in Guangzhou. I had no way of knowing if this was true, but it wasn't what was important. What mattered was his voice was genuinely good, that's what warmed me to him.

Before we started drinking, he explained that the trip had been an impromptu decision. His girlfriend had broken up with him and he needed some distraction. I consoled him, as you do, the usual – this must have been his fourth breakup, and there's only so much you can say to comfort a person. But, after a few cups, I thought I'd test the waters.

"You still in a group?"

"Not any more. Work won't give me the time off."

"But you still practise? Flex the vocal cords?"

"Of course."

"Ah well," I exhaled. "You must be a bit shaken right now, but remember, this sort of thing happens. What are you going to do? Forget her. Do you think it might help if you try to sing a little? It's good for the heart, I've heard."

The wife was bringing in dishes at that exact moment and shot me a warning look before sitting down at the table herself.

"I'm not in the mood," he grumbled as he reached for the bottle.

I snatched it from the table before his hand could close around it, then turned to the wife. "You go cook in the kitchen," I said.

"And you leave alone. You've got your food, now eat it," she said.

"The men are talking. Don't you be causing trouble, woman."

The wife stayed put.

"Come on, sing something," I said, patting the in-law's shoulder. "I like hearing you sing."

Head bowed, looking into his cup, he was quiet. Then his head tipped back and he started to sing.

My heart felt like an old sailboat
that had sailed its last rough sea...

I didn't know the song, but that was fine. I've long thought that lyrics aren't what make a tune, it's how it sounds that counts. And boy, could he sing. It wasn't that he was belting it – how should I put this? I'm no music expert – his voice could just move a man. I sat there with a serious look on my face, so he knew I was listening, and also because I was preparing myself to sing next. I hoped he would return the favour of a fitting response. Listening to someone else sing is all well and good, it really is, but there's nothing I like more than having others listen to me.

"Bravo, bravo."

I made sure to lay it on thick when he finished. I then took a swig of my drink to wet the throat and puffed up my chest to project better. "Now it's my turn. Listen to this," I said.

"I ought to have guessed," said the wife. Her expression said she knew what was coming. She turned and said to her brother, "Ignore the old man. One drink and he's suddenly a crooner. Only he sounds more like a braying donkey. Have you heard a donkey before?"

"I haven't. Let him sing."

"Nope, no way. We're not letting him sing. I've got experience. The drinking is just a pretext, he's always looking for an excuse to start his wailing."

I chose to ignore her. I was too used to her tongue wagging by then. I tried to think of a tune I knew well. The passion for singing I had right there, at the ready.

I had just licked my lips and was about to launch into song when the door opened. Fatso Li our neighbour walked in.

"Who was singing?" he asked as he blustered into the room.

It was the in-law's voice that brought him over. Fatso liked to hum himself in a spare moment at home.

He instantly ruined my appetite. I closed my mouth.

The wife introduced her brother. Li was very chummy and plonked himself down right beside my in-law like they were best pals. Sending spittle everywhere, he started whistling a tune and explaining intonation to the in-law.

"...that's it, now match that with your chest voice... right, there we go. The bass is down in the stomach. I've been practising this for a few days now..."

The wife seemed to have forgotten about me for the time being. Her attention had been seized by the spittle spraying from Fatso Li's mouth, for fear it might land on the food. I wasn't bothered in the slightest, nor did I get a word of what Fatso was babbling on about. I sat there bored.

Fucking shit, I thought, Fatso Li mouthing off about chest voice this, stomach voice that, it must be because he's got the tits of a woman and the belly of a pig. If there was a monkey around, no doubt he'd be extolling the virtues of using your tail to harmonise. He's spouting bullshit.

Brother-in-Law was a bit like that, though. He'd never heard the man sing, and his ears were still pricked to listen to this inane drivel.

I filled my glass and knocked it back in one.

"What a tipple!" I growled, extra loud.

Fatso Li almost jumped out of his seat. His jaw was swinging in surprise, which put an end to the spraying spittle. The three of them looked at me.

"Brother, singing's about technique," said the in-law.

"Pah, technique."

"Right, we're not talking technique today." He must have noticed the look in my eye. He poured Fatso a drink, probably to keep him quiet. "Come on then, Brother. Give us a tune."

"That's more like it." I had my second wave, all of a sudden.

"Hold on," said the wife, still standing. "I'll do the beat."

She took a chopstick from the table and traced an arc in the air, then paused. She gave me a nod.

With one swipe, I slapped the chopstick out of her hand, sending it flying. I had half a mind to go for her face.

The room went silent.

Perfect. I wasn't picky about atmosphere. If no one wanted to hear me sing when they were being all jolly, then I would sing through the awkwardness.

As long as they were going to be quiet and listen, I was content.

There was an old man who spent his days by the sea,
Gazing up at the blue, gazing down at the green.
It was his favourite thing to gather babes all around,
And tell his best tales of life in the town

......

Oo-aah... he caught himself a whopper.
Oo-aah... he cau-ght him-self a who-pper.

I had barely got going when the wife stood up and

walked out of the room, like she had remembered something she had forgotten. Meanwhile, Fatso Li wore this awful strange grin the whole time I was singing.

None of this helped my mood. But I quickly let go of any distracting thoughts and put my all into the singing. It's how I've always done it.

When I finished the song, I was a bit out of breath but feeling much better. I couldn't tell if they had noticed the long, wobbly note I put at the end. I ate two pieces of meat, settled myself down and looked at the in-law. "How about that?"

"Huh." I couldn't read the look he was giving me. It was like I'd said something I shouldn't have. "Well, it was worth a listen."

"Bollocks. It had no rhythm." This was Fatso Li.

"He is right, to be fair. There was no sense of rhythm. You didn't draw out the right parts, but then you went for it in odd places."

Rhythm, schmythm. I don't sing to show off that I can count.

"Can you learn rhythm?" I asked anyway.

"Afraid not. It's something you're born with."

Born with it. Got it. I had got it years earlier, too, though. This was while I was in middle school, when they put out the annual call to the city's schools for applicants for pilot training. I passed the first checks, and at the next stage the doctors put those of us who had progressed together in this big room, then put us in groups of three and had each group, one by one, strip naked in the middle of the space. In front of seven or eight doctors and everyone else there, we were ordered to march, butt naked, to a count.

When it got to my turn, me and the two guys in my group marched up and down the room twice. A doctor then asked the other two to get changed again and left me standing there.

"Do you want to be a pilot or not?" another doctor asked.

"I really do." I answered like I thought I should.

"Then why did you march out of stride?"

"It wasn't on purpose."

"OK, you'll do two more lengths, following my count. Attention. March! One two, one two, one two, one... Halt! You can leave."

"Why?"

"You have no natural rhythm, that's why."

I thought it best to ask Brother-in-Law, "Are you saying I'll never learn to sing?"

"Why do you want to so bad?" he replied.

"I've got a nice voice."

"Then you're best doing it someplace where there's no one else around," said Fatso Li. He was proud of this barb and scooped up his glass for a celebratory drink.

"It's always singing this, singing that," said the wife.

"The food's going cold, eat up." Who knows when she had come back in.

"Let's do a song together. The four of us," the in-law suggested.

"We'll be a choir." Fatso was on board.

"OK, but you'll eat after we're done," said the wife.

So the in-law started singing, and we all joined in.

I listened to their voices: the in-law's was low and bassy, the wife's scratchy, and Fatso's was booming. He was singing the loudest out of all of us. Probably his voice could resonate in the big jumble of intestines that must fill his ginormous paunch, before it reached the outside, like he was a hi-fi system. The only voice I couldn't hear was my own. I stood up and slipped out. After pissing, I lingered in the bathroom a moment. I glanced around me. Then I started to sing, really quietly, the song about the old man and the sea:

There was an old man who spent his days by the sea...
Oo-aah... he caught himself a whopper
Oooo-aah... he cau-ght him-self a who-pper

My muted voice echoed inside the small bathroom. There was no one around to listen.

America Story

Wang Lu was back from the States for two months before I finally decided to see him. Which isn't proper, really, I know. We were old friends, classmates at university, and we had stayed close in the twelve years since. But this had nothing to do with being cold-hearted or fickle, that's not why I didn't welcome him back straight away. It was because of a foible of mine: stupidity is something I struggle to tolerate, especially that of my friends. Experience has shown me that anyone who goes to America comes back impossibly stupid. It doesn't matter how sharp they were beforehand, and it doesn't matter how short-lived it is, it still gets my goat. They come back talking like they visited the capital city of humankind, the world's epicentre. They chat to their fellow countrymen like we're underfed yokels who wouldn't know a good meal if it slapped us in the face. It's that look they have that irks me, like they honestly believe they've seen the greatest show on earth. A lifetime ago, when I was still in nursery, our teacher took our top-set class on a trip to the city stadium to watch a circus performance. The last act was tigers jumping through flaming hoops. Every time a tiger, at the crack of the tamer's whip, leapt through a great big hula hoop of fire, all of us kids would jump up and down and cheer. But nowadays I can't get remotely excited about tricks like that, it makes no difference if the tiger is American or Chinese.

* * *

I headed over after dinner, just before dusk. I walked. That way I would get some exercise and it was easier to take my time – like I said, I wasn't thrilled at the prospect of seeing Wang Lu right then.

Along the way, at Xinjiekou, I saw a man who was clearly from the countryside standing on the pavement under a large neon sign. He was wearing a dirty yellow padded jacket, even though it was warm out, and blue cotton trousers. He had a flowery bedroll in one hand, and in the other a plastic woven tote with a cord handle. He looked like he was in a hurry to ask someone for directions, but like he'd been cowed by the bustling city streets, and the courage to open his mouth and ask had gone from him. The poor fellow was glancing between passers-by, with something like panic in his eyes.

A young boy, who must have been his son, was squatting next to him. The kid was maybe three or four years old and wearing open-crotch trousers for doing his business easily. He was covered in dust. With a chubby little digit, he was diligently prodding at some ants on the ground, while the softening dusk light shining on his head lit him up a dull green and, for a brief moment, the din of the city gave way to quiet. I stopped walking. There was something in that boy's calm that moved me.

I got to Wang Lu's place just as it was getting dark.

Wang Lu was happy to see me, patting me on the shoulder and calling for his wife Xiao Song to pour some tea while complaining that I hadn't come sooner. He clearly hadn't thought that coming to mine was an option. In the lounge, I found there was someone else there. A pretty woman, thirty-ish, with this high forehead and tanned skin. Her hair was combed back in a ponytail and she looked a lot like one of the singers who had become big some years earlier. She wore a low-cut, black wool jumper, and she sat up perfectly straight on the sofa. I took in her slender figure, waiting for Wang Lu to make the introductions. Whatever happened next, meeting a pretty woman like her was always going to make for a much more interesting time, even if it did end with having to listen to him blabber on about America. But all he said was that I was a friend of his. Then turning to the woman, as if to assure her, he said, "He has serious feelings for you, really. He was always telling me how much he misses you. I'm not exaggerating." The woman blushed. She was touched.

"But..." she looked about to say something but then remembered I was there and swallowed the words. She started fidgeting in her seat like my presence made her uncomfortable. She stood up and said she was leaving. Wang Lu seemed happy to let her go, too, but Xiao Song said, "Sit down, stay a little longer, it's no bother." Then, pointing at me, she said, "He's an old friend." I appreciated her saying this, but the woman insisted on going anyway.

Wang Lu saw her off, then came back in shaking his head, a helpless look on his face. "Her husband is in America. We get along well," he said. "He's a real charmer. It only took him five minutes before he was hooking up with two locals. But she's still holding out hope that he'll fly her over there once he's settled in. Real dim, that one."

"What are you going on about?" Xiao Song grumbled at him. "She's already had a hard enough time as it is."

I thought she had a point. Tragedies like this happen every day and no one can do anything about it. "Wang

Lu, you've put on weight," I said. It was true. He looked much healthier than a year ago. Even his cheeks were rosy now. But his hair did have grey coming through.

Wang Lu grinned at me and touched his creasing cheeks. "I know, everyone says the same. I tried to look after myself over there. I started every day with fruit juice and some vitamins. In America, your health matters most. If you get sick, you're done for, especially if you're not earning. Doctor's fees are scary high. I didn't catch a cold even once over there, can you believe that?"

I could. But then, I would happily believe whatever he wanted me to, that he had made a million dollars or lived on the streets begging. The secret was that I didn't care.

"How are things with you?" Xiao Song asked. "Got a girlfriend yet?"

"I've got a few," I said.

Xiao Song scoffed with surprise. "Well, I just don't know why you and Yang Hongyan divorced in the first place," she said, a moment later. "I liked her, and she was good for you. I heard she's single again, I reckon you should get back together."

I leant back on the sofa. "I agree she's a good person, I still think that to this day. She's kind, and earnest, and smart, at that. If only she didn't cheat on her husband. Just wait until I've conquered my baser desires and I'm fed up with single life. I'll think about it, then. But I've no plans for that anytime soon, I'm enjoying being single."

Wang Lu slapped his thigh. "Damn right," he said, a little too loudly. "Everyone ought to live however feels best. Nothing else matters. That's the American view. What's stuck with me most after so long over there is that Americans don't hold anything back, they put it all out there. One time I was in this bookshop and there was a black guy bent down browsing the lower shelves, and he was wearing his jeans like black guys always do in America, hanging halfway down their arse, and when he bent down further, the jeans slipped a little more, and suddenly I was staring at these big, round arse cheeks. No underwear. But the guy didn't care. He didn't even pull them up or try to cover himself. He just kept on browsing the books. Everyone else acted like it was the most normal thing in the world. They didn't look twice. I'm telling you, I've never seen an arse like that up close before. It shocked me. Another time, I saw this group gathered on a street corner, 'Society for the Prevention of the Spread of HIV/AIDS' or something like that. They had a big banner with 'What if Clinton got HIV?' in red on it. Under the writing there was a massive red condom, and I bet you can guess what was under it..."

I took the box of Wanbaolu cigarettes from the

coffee table and lit one, and while I smoked I looked over at Wang Lu's face. It was obvious he was excited. This was the face of a forty-year-old man, full, ruddy, shiny with grease, a few duller spots where his colour was fading, purple bags forming under his eyes. It wouldn't be too many years before this face would slacken and become ugly. We all grow old one day. And what will excite us then? Already, our bolder life decisions didn't seem worth mentioning any more... So I'll mention something here that Wang Lu did about ten years before, when we were day students in the history department at Nanjing Uni. Wang Lu was living in west Nanjing then and, his family having no money to give him for travel, he fare-skipped on the bus in and back every day. He got pretty good at it, too, and was always boasting about this trick he came up with for getting away with it. I can't remember what the trick was now, but he eventually made a mistake and was caught by the ticket inspector, and because he couldn't pay the fine which was ten times the ticket price, he was dragged all the way to the depot. When they got him there, he started screaming, "Aren't you humans too? Do you have no heart? Where's your compassion?" But his big mouth only earned him a beating, and he was black and blue by the time someone from the school arrived to fetch him.

Apparently, his view of people was fundamentally changed after that.

* * *

"If you've got money, there's no better place to live than America." This was his big conclusion. He had just been saying how fresh and fragrant the air was in America since the department for environmental protection had put measures in to block all channels of pollution, and how thorough and conscientious the social welfare services were, how if your phone company overcharged you even one cent and an investigation confirmed it, then the company had to send someone to your door to personally apologise. All tosh.

It was at this point that Xiao Song, who had been slipping lower and lower down the sofa with a pinched expression, hid a yawn and then stood up. "I'll see how the boy's doing with his homework," she said.

She headed into the inner bedroom. I felt for Xiao Song. I could only imagine how many dozens of times she had heard Wang Lu say these same things over and over with all the people coming round to see him. Of course she wanted to escape. I was lucky by comparison. But that didn't mean I was ready to let Wang Lu jabber on unchecked. I looked at my watch. "I'm off."

Wang Lu reached over and put his hand on my shoulder. "What's the hurry? It's still early."

I stood up, though I didn't really have the heart to leave, and said, "I've got a thing. We'll see each other soon." In my head, I followed this with, Maybe we should wait though, friend.

* * *

All the same, I was sitting in front of him again only a week later. He had called me and asked, "You free tonight?" He sounded knackered, and like something was up. "Can I come to yours?"

I thought about it and said, "If you get here early, I'll take you to dinner." I hung up. Then I dialled the number of the woman I was supposed to see later that evening and cancelled.

Wang Lu turned up a little past five. He looked pale and frustrated, a changed man from the gasbag of the week before, like maybe he had regained some of his sense of reality. About bloody time, I thought. Who in this life can be so chipper all the time, unless they're simple?

Sitting down, Wang Lu glanced around the room. "It looks the same as before."

"Dirty and a mess," he added.

"It's not so bad," I said.

"Don't you ever tidy up? It's good for the mind, you know."

"My mind is just fine."

"No, it's not. You've got no drive."

I smiled. I was not going to argue with him. We valued different things – but it didn't stop us being friends. I would never go to America, for example, not with a gun to my head. The country could unanimously vote me its president and I still wouldn't go. Or I might, but only to announce my first and only decree: the United States is disbanded. "You sound like you've got something on your mind," I said, changing topic. "What's up?"

"You noticed," he said. "This week's been rubbish."

He paused, then told me what happened. His university, where he was a history lecturer, had notified him that if he left the country again, he would have to surrender the flat that it had assigned him. He couldn't let that happen, because where would his wife and kid go? The implication was clear: the university didn't want him going abroad. It was a blow, he said, he had worked hard to establish his network over there and he was getting a decent wage now his reputation was growing. He guested as a professor of Chinese, and these things took time. "You know how difficult it is to get your name out there." His plan had been to come back and build up to renewing his agreement with the university here before making off again. And now this. What a fucking kick in the teeth.

"Can't you take them with you?" I asked.

"Not at this point."

"Anyone who could pull some strings for you?"

"Honestly, I've tried everyone. I haven't stopped trying. But the school's answer is final. There are explicit terms about this sort of thing, from higher up, so there's little chance of getting around them." Wang Lu sighed and his face settled into a frown as he sat there in silence.

I didn't know what to tell him that might be helpful or reassuring. We sat there quietly for a long moment, then I said we should eat.

We went to the small place I like on the nearby crossroad.

The waitresses knew me well and one in particular, Zhang Min, a curvy lady from the province's north, had a thing for me I was sure. I was always joking with her that we should get married. When we went in, it was Zhang Min who saw us and came over. "Mr Gu," she said, "it's been days, where've you been hiding?"

"Did you miss me?"

She gave me a coquettish look, then took us to a table. I handed Wang Lu the menu so he could order but he waved it away, so I picked out a few things and got beers too.

The food didn't take long to arrive. Zhang Min poured our drinks. "Wang Lu," I said, pointing at Zhang Min. "This woman is my future wife." Wang Lu looked her up and down.

"You've got taste," he said.

"Mr Gu is a joker." She was putting on a flirty voice. Our glasses full, she left us for a moment then came back with placemats and toothpicks. It got me wondering whether she might actually like me. One time I was there and no one else was looking, I gave her arse a squeeze, and since then, she had always hovered around me as if I was on my own. I obviously didn't do anything more than that. I didn't want this poor country girl getting any unrealistic ideas about us.

"Zhang Min," I said, "this man here has just come back from America. You look after him, OK? Show this weary traveller some of the motherland's warmth."

"Here's to him, then." Zhang Min picked up my glass and clinked it against Wang Lu's, and the pair downed their drinks. Wetting her lips suggestively, she put the glass back in front of me and refilled Wang Lu's. Someone in the kitchen called for her and she scuttled off.

"She's forward," Wang Lu said, blinking at me.

"Anything like American girls?" I raised my glass and tapped it against thin air.

Wang Lu raised his, too, and took a big swig.

"American girls aren't nearly as laidback as everyone thinks they are. At least, the ones I've met aren't." His forehead was flushing red. Whether it was the alcohol or the America-talk, he was perking up quickly. "I mean, fuck. If you ask me, it's our women over there who are the odd ones."

"Is that right?" I said. "Eat, eat."

"Yes, listen to this. I'll tell you about this Shanghai girl." Wang Lu put a piece of braised pig's intestine into his mouth and started to chew as he spoke.

I thought he was going to tell me some dirty story, so I smiled at him encouragingly.

* * *

"So back when I first went over there and didn't have a good job yet, I got by doing deliveries for takeaways. Do you know what that is? Right, a lot of hard work. But from dropping off food at theirs a few times, I got to know this Chinese couple who lived in state-subsidised housing. A flat on the first floor. It was a tip, to be honest. The guy, Yao, was an old fellow, and Sun, his wife, was much younger, and not bad-looking either. I think seeing a Chinese face, they wanted to chat with me, though mostly it was Yao. We got to know each other pretty well, anyway. Then, eventually, I turned up on a few occasions, in the evening like always, and Yao would have gone out, for a walk or whatever, and Sun, the woman, would start getting *really* friendly with me, leaning against the doorframe, that kind of thing. She never asked me inside, probably in case the old man ever found out. But I came to know a fair bit about their lives.

"Yao was eighty-one, even if he only looked in his sixties. He had some colour to his face and good posture. Nothing like the doddering old man you imagine. He was from Shandong and had been a commander in the Kuomintang for an artillery regiment. He fought against the Japanese and was awarded a medal for outstanding military service. After the war, he moved from Taiwan to America, where he worked as a handyman in a bunch of middle schools until he retired. He had three sons and two daughters, all in America and with families and careers. But they never visited the old man. His wife had died some years before from illness.

"Sun was thirty-nine. Thirty. Nine. She was from Shanghai and hadn't been there for a year. She had been introduced to Yao while she was still in Shanghai. She was divorced. When I asked her about Yao, she said he was as crafty as they come. The first time they met, when he went over from America to see her, he knew he liked her straight away, but because it was too soon to bring up marriage, he bought her some gold jewellery and told her that he didn't have anything on, and he was in no hurry to get back to the States, so why didn't they book into a cheap room in Shanghai for the night. She wasn't stupid, of course. So she tried to give him a fright: 'That won't do, that's called illegal cohabitation here. It'll get you arrested.' The guy had no choice, he had to ask her to marry him. That got her to America, anyway. But life had been disappointing since then, she said – nothing to do with America, who could be disappointed with that place? It was Yao. He was always telling her, because she didn't speak English, that getting around would be difficult, and Americans are terrible people. A woman like her who couldn't speak the language, she would get swindled. Or abducted and thrown in some brothel. So she had been in America all that time and hardly gone outside. They were in Washington and she'd never even seen the White House. And the old man only ever let her read the same book over and over, a classic text on *Womanly Virtue*. And he only ever thumbed through the same copy of *The Three Principles of the People*. She had had enough of only reading one book during the Cultural Revolution, she said, she didn't think she'd be lumped with the same fate in the States. She was laughing as she told me this, but I could tell she was bitter. Yao didn't have any friends and he hardly ever saw anyone. He liked to drink. And when he did, he would always tell her the same story about his time as a school janitor when he would mop the toilets and find condoms all over the floor. Like this was the one thing from his past that had stayed with him.

"Once, when I dropped a delivery off, Sun said that she was bored with life. I told her to stick it out just a little longer. The old man was already eighty, he couldn't have much more life in him.

"She disagreed. He ate well, she said, he had lots of energy and was still strong. She knew. He hit her. There was one time a neighbour called round, a guy in his sixties, and though she barely said a word to him, Yao still beat her when he had gone. She couldn't get out of bed for three days after.

"I flinched when she told me. So the old man was as jealous as that. I caught myself peering down the steps all of a sudden scared he might appear.

"And that's not even the worst thing, she said.

"But then she stopped and didn't go on. Her face went bright red. And out it all came, all this anger and resentment she had been keeping down. She spilled it all. Apparently, Old Man Yao liked to have two sleeps a day. From noon until four, then from ten at night until six in the morning. And she had to sleep with him every time, naked, and spooning him. And if she got tired doing that, then he'd let her face him, pressed right up close. She wasn't allowed to sleep on her back or face away from him, and if she tried to roll over he would hit her. She said she never slept at night, and it was worse during the day. She started crying when she got to this point. 'I can't take it any more, no one should have to go through this.'

"And she was right. Picture them lying next to each other. It sends a shiver through me. But I didn't feel much sympathy for her, to be honest. There's this saying in America, No such thing as a free lunch. This was the price she was paying for the food on her plate. Everyone has one. Me, I'm a university lecturer, but in America I was a delivery driver. I even did some labouring here and there. I didn't think there was anything wrong with that, though. It was fair, it made sense. She had nothing to complain about either. It's the same with so many Chinese women, they reckon they're so charming and wherever they go they can solve all their problems with a little flirting and acting spoiled.

"But America isn't falling for it. America is the sort of place where–"

"What happened next?" I said, cutting him off.

"When next?"

"With Sun."

"I'm getting there, be patient." He reached for a beer bottle to refill his glass but they were all empty.

I turned in my seat and saw Zhang Min leaning against the wall nearby. I waved.

"Two more beers."

Zhang Min was over in a flash, pouring us out a beer

each and throwing me expectant glances because I wasn't saying anything. Glasses filled, she left us be, reluctantly. "She's got her eye on you," Wang Lu said.

"Maybe. You keep going."

* * *

"I found something else to do soon after that. No more deliveries, and I never saw Sun again. I thought about going round sometimes, but things got busy and I couldn't find the time, and I was unsure about that Yao fellow now I knew what he was like. About six months later, I bumped into him outside a shop. He was sat on the step in a big coat, enjoying the sun. I called to him and he just stared, like he didn't recognise me. I told him who I was, and he grunted a few times. I asked how're things, how's the wife. That was like I'd poked a hornet's nest. He jumped to his feet with all the agility no one his age ought to have, and grabbed me and started shouting about 'that ungrateful witch'. I said he shouldn't get angry, just say slowly what happened. That only started him off again. But he told me the whole tale, eventually. Three months before, she had told him she wanted to go home to see her daughter. He had said no. But then she pestered him and wore him down and he agreed, giving her fifteen hundred dollars for the trip. Then she said that clothes are cheap in China, she'll bring some back for him. Which made the old man happy, so he gave her two hundred bucks more. Cut to a few days after she's gone, and he calls her long-distance to ask when she'll be back, but what do you know? They said at the other end that she never came back. She just disappeared, like a clay ox in the sea. And he still hadn't had any news. 'Deceitful fox.' He was spitting feathers.

"I wasn't exactly a fan of the guy, so I was thinking that it served him right, but I said my bit to calm him down, then made my exit. I'm still not sure if he ever recognised who I was."

* * *

When we left the eatery and before parting ways, Wang Lu and I arranged to meet up again in a few days.

Afterwards, I stopped not far down the path, thinking about the lives of Sun and Yao on the other side of the planet. All the trivia and boring parts of them, the mundanity. About how we're all powerless against the void. I thought about this, standing there a moment. Then I headed home.

Hello, Postman

It was not by choice that Xu Liang went to Haikou. He was not a fan of hard work and he wasn't ambitious, plus he had a stable job already as an electrician in a radio factory, and though the pay wasn't great, his life was trouble-free. To all intents and purposes, a man like him was playing his part by leading a modest existence, and that was what he had planned to do. If it wasn't for Wang Hong, he would have had no reason to leave home and try to make things work in Haikou. The couple had been married for two years at that point. It was just the two of them still, and there was real warmth and love there. Wang Hong was an accountant-slash-typist at a neighbourhood copy shop, and on any given day, with all the people coming in to print cultural materials, she served a good number of quite accomplished folk. Though whether it was these interactions that shaped Wang Hong's outlook was hard to say. It could just as well have been that she was never happy to live an ordinary life, not that this would have been a mark against her, it's perfectly understandable if a young woman longs for days with a bit more shine to them. But it meant that she started whispering in Xu Liang's ear. The long and short of it was that she wished Xu Liang had more get-up-and-go, more spunk. They couldn't just settle for things as they were, there was more to life than that, so why didn't he have a stab at starting a career while he still had youth on his side?

Naturally, Xu Liang was unlikely to go changing his ways all because of a little grumbling. A man of character, intrepid and self-sacrificing, he was not. Still, he considered the idea. He had a strong sense of responsibility and wanted his woman to have the life of her dreams. At the very least, she should have the things that others had. And being so amiable, he was easily talked around, especially when it was the woman he loved doing the talking. After an intense battle of minds, Xu Liang eventually agreed to find himself a career.

But in what? The factory offered no prospects. He could work there until he died and still be doing the same tasks, day in, day out. Landing a job at a good company with development potential, though, was even more of a pipe dream. Xu Liang had no qualifications beyond sixth form, and no half-decent place was going to accept someone without a degree, unless he was happy watching the gate or mopping the toilets. Open a shop himself, then? He would need money to do that. There was always the option to start a shell company, of course, if he were OK with committing fraud. Husband and wife batted ideas back and forth and eventually concluded that the only option was to go to Hainan. The island had recently been made a Special Economic Zone and there were lots of preferential policies to be taken advantage of which were not available on the mainland. Lots of regulations were still under discussion, or in the gradual process of being consolidated. Basically, there was opportunity aplenty, and he had heard no end of stories of people moving there and making good. So why shouldn't Xu Liang try his luck?

He got his request approved for leave without pay, then dashed off for the island's provincial capital, Haikou. Saying goodbye beforehand was difficult for the young couple, and for Xu Liang in particular, who ached at the thought of living so far apart. Like in that song:

When we say goodbye to the one we love, aaa-aah aa-ah,
To go somewhere far away, and in our hea-aaah-ah-arts,
Oh, we feel so much pain...

He did a year there, and then some, trying his hand

at a variety of trades. He sold car tyres, mixed lights and sound for a club, hawked vintage clothes at a night market, managed a speaker store at an electronics market, sold ads for a newspaper. Those were some hard months. Anyone with a little life experience will relate to the struggle that comes with establishing yourself away from home. But when things got really tough, he knew that he could always turn to thoughts of Wang Hong for relief. This was why, on most nights, he wrote her a letter.

How sweet he was: hunched over the desk after a long day of work baring his soul to his beloved Wang Hong, writing and writing and sometimes finding himself so worked up a teardrop might drip onto the paper. Did Wang Hong ever notice the tear stains on the page? What commitment he showed, how moving. But in the twelve months-plus he was there, did he see any success? I won't beat around the bush: the answer is no. In fact, he was even worse off than before. When he left for the island he had at least had three thousand socked away, and some treasury securities to boot. He lived frugally in Haikou, too, sending home in instalments the five thousand he had sweated and bled to earn. Only, when he returned home a year and a bit later, every last cent of it was gone. Xu Liang had worked himself ragged and ended up a pauper.

So, with skin now as dark as donkey shit from baking

under the tropical sun of Haikou, and several kilos lighter, he toiled with gritted teeth in the name of his wife's happiness, on and on. And then a letter arrived from Wang Hong. The letter didn't say much beyond, simply, that he ought to go home right away so she could divorce him. Xu Liang didn't know what had happened. In shock, he did exactly as he was told, not wanting to waste a minute more. Waiting at home to greet him was a frosty-faced Wang Hong. Her reason for wanting a divorce: being apart so long, her feelings had waned, and she didn't want to be married to him any more. Xu Liang didn't understand. Was the long-term separation not Wang Hong's idea? He had even planned to go back to see her over Spring Festival and she hadn't let him, saying in her reply then that a return trip was expensive, he was better off saving on the expenses and sending the money to her. He had to put his all into making it in Haikou, she said, and anyway, they would have many more days together in the future once he had. Yet now their separation was grounds for divorce? It made no sense.

But that was apparently beside the point since Wang Hong gave no other reason. She was staying firm, there was no room for discussion. Xu Liang had to agree to the divorce. When it came to dividing assets, she was laid back. The only thing she wanted was a clean start. Their place had been Xu Liang's before they married, and the little furniture they owned was worthless. But a clean start, in this case, meant that all the savings Xu Liang had sent home, plus his securities, were cleaned out.

It was a while later that Xu Liang finally learned the true reason for the divorce. His neighbours all knew it before he did, and had been chewing the matter over ever since. He was always going to find out, sooner or later. Xu Liang's place was in an old part of the city, down an alley with more than a hundred years of history. The houses down there were mostly drab-looking, squat single-storeys with shared courtyards, some big some small. The residents were a bit all over the place and rarely did they have a communal mailbox, so when the postman came he would stand in the courtyard and holler for the recipient to come out, then hand the mail to whoever appeared. If no one did, he would stuff the mail under their door. Not long after Xu Liang went to Haikou, the usual postal worker who worked his alley took maternity leave and a young lad replaced her. Delivery time was normally around five in the afternoon, which was just as Wang Hong got back from work. His neighbours told Xu Liang that Wang Hong had started to receive an awful lot of letters, with a new one arriving almost daily. At first, the young lad would hand the letters over to her, then go. But after a while, the pair got talking. Just the usual to start with, but then they moved on to joking with each other and chatting away. Later still, the lad would drop off the letters then stick around and hang out, maybe even stay for dinner. Now, sharing a yard means that everyone is in everyone else's business, neighbours as good as live on top of each other, so a person only had to open their window to see into next door. The neighbours said that when it came to hosting her guest, Wang Hong pulled out all the stops, laying out tablesful of good dishes for him and buying in drinks. Then early one morning, still in the haze of dawn, an early riser saw the young lad sneaking out of Wang Hong's. That was right, the neighbours said, Wang Hong had even gone away twice, for two weeks each time, and when they asked where she had been, she would say Haikou, to see her husband. But had she gone to see him? Xu Liang said absolutely not. More probable was that she had gone on a trip with the young postman. Taking Xu Liang's hard-earned money and enjoying a getaway with her lover. So Wang Hong was capable of such things.

"What's he look like?" Xu Liang asked. Before he had hurried back from Haikou, the original postie had had her child and started back at work, so he had never seen the young replacement.

"Tall," his neighbours said. "And fair. Good skin."

It was clear what had happened. Xu Liang's treasured memories of Wang Hong had got him cuckolded and led to their divorce. Just think, if Xu Liang hadn't been so caught up on her or had managed to keep his thoughts on the right side of obsessive, only thought of her occasionally, for instance, or maybe less intensely, then would things have really turned out the same? He wouldn't have written her a letter nearly every day, that's for sure. Maybe one a month, or one a week, at most. Which would have meant that slippery postman wouldn't have needed to see Wang Hong so often, and well, isn't it possible he wouldn't have hooked her? It's true, the culprit here was Xu's own obsession, and it was too late for him now to repent. If she had never even entered his head, she probably wouldn't have met the postman, never mind been corrupted by him. Xu Liang could even imagine a world in which Wang Hong was in no rush to open the letters delivered by that bastard, and maybe even waited until the two of them were finished in bed before she would open one of them and the pair would lay with their heads side by side on the pillow and make fun of his heartfelt words, or the tear stains on the page. And if all that laughing happened to get them in the mood again, then they'd go back at it. It was all too painful to imagine. What sort of person would do this?

Xu Liang told his neighbours that he wanted to see the young guy. To them, this sounded like he was after revenge, which was music to their ears. No one should get away with such sordid behaviour, where would be the justice? One neighbour took it upon himself to give the guy up, volunteering to take Xu Liang to the post office and point him out. He said he had been there himself only a few days before and spotted him. So off they went.

The post office was busy, with customers crammed in shoulder to shoulder all facing in the direction of the counter. The neighbour gave a sign and whispered, "See him? The one taking the money there." The guy was really young, twenty-two or twenty-three at a push, and he looked just like the neighbours had said, fair and with good skin. Beyond that, he had a wide forehead and high nose, thick black hair which looked naturally curly. He was, to be completely honest, quite the looker.

Was Xu Liang really out for revenge? He had thought about it, but that was all. Violence wasn't really in his nature, and what's more, he felt sort of sorry for Wang Hong; he could see how a good-looking lad like him might turn the head of a young woman living alone. And when he got to the bottom of it, he was the one who had written so many letters. From then on, if Xu Liang had any reason to go to the post office, he would always stand to one side and stare quietly at the young buck behind the counter, while wondering to himself whether he and Wang Hong were still doing it or perhaps even living together. How was their relationship?

Then almost a year later, Xu Liang had to go to the

post office for something and the guy was nowhere to be seen. He must have been transferred to another branch.

* * *

Fast forward twenty years later still, and Xu Liang was unrecognisable from his former scruffy self. People now called him "Boss" or "Mr Xu".

What had happened was that he never went back to his old job at the radio factory. He was too ashamed to do that. He had left to make his fortune and returned broke and wifeless. Luckily for him, the Electricity Board had recently opened up a position for a transmission worker, a gruelling and high-risk job that no one wanted. But Xu Liang didn't have any connections elsewhere, and there was no simply walking into a job at a good company, plus he was qualified for the role thanks to his electrician's licence, so it was his only decent option. And though the prospects were few to none, Xu Liang was a hard worker and dependable, and gradually he managed to carve out a reputation. First, he was promoted to transmission team lead. This was also when he started at night school, where three years later he would receive his associate degree. Then he became deputy section chief of production technology. And then section chief. And then section chief of power usage. And vice director of the Electric Board. Then director. And when the Electric Board became a utility company, he moved to the municipal headquarters to serve as vice president.

By then, the company could promise better benefits. With the state monopolising the industry, wages were higher and employees were treated well, and without a solid connection on the inside, there was no way in. But Xu Liang was in, and on the up. In only his second year at the Electric Board, someone introduced him to a decent and considerate woman who worked in the finance department, and the new couple soon had a daughter together. That daughter recently started her graduate research at a university in another province.

Xu Liang would still occasionally think of his first wife, but always with that same pity as before. He had slowly pieced together what had happened to Wang Hong from scraps of news fed to him by a shared friend. She moved to Shanghai, then Shenzhen, and lived with various men along the way. Some of those men apparently came to blows in fits of jealousy. She then went abroad, though it was unclear where, and her messages stopped. She seemed to have no direction, and it was not hard to imagine that her days were difficult. But who else was there to blame?

These thoughts also brought to mind the young fair-faced postman. Of course they did. Mostly Xu Liang felt gratitude to the guy. If that young man had never appeared in his life, then Wang Hong and Xu Liang might not have divorced. It frightened him to think! He knew full well the type of person Wang Hong was now, and by that he didn't mean good or bad, just that, for a husband, she was a car crash waiting to happen. And who had thrown themselves in front of Xu Liang if not the young postman?

And if the postman had never barged into Xu Liang's life, Xu Liang would never even have joined the Electric Board, never mind everything that followed. In some way, Xu Liang owed his whole life to the guy. It's strange how things work sometimes. No one knows when an apparent disaster might suddenly become a blessing. Or when the best thing that ever happened to you will turn out the opposite.

Xu Liang, though, was doing OK. He and his wife sold their apartment in the city and bought a 280 square metre semi-detached house with three floors out in Fairgarden, a fashionable neighbourhood in the east suburbs. The neighbourhood backed onto a hilly range and had a gorgeous lake in front. The place was fully furnished and had access to all the facilities they would need. There was a gym, primary school, nursery, supermarket, restaurants, allotments, a doctor's, a post office. Xu Liang had no plans to ever leave. He felt like he had everything in order and he had zero regrets.

Then one Saturday, early on in this new chapter of

life, after finishing lunch, and while his wife was sorting their belongings and tidying up at their new home, Xu Liang headed to the post office to post their daughter some clothes his wife had just bought for her. He stepped out of the door and took the quiet, tree-lined path towards the complex's gate.

The new neighbourhood was still barely occupied and he passed very few people on the streets. Out of the gate, he turned right into the recently finished commercial area. The post office was at the end of a line of shops. Xu Liang pushed open the door and went in. The interior was clean and well-organised, with a large window letting in plenty of light and warmth. He could see no other customers waiting. Maybe the notion of a lunchtime rush didn't apply there. Sat behind the marble counter was a young woman who looked about ready to nod off, and at the other end, a portly man of middle age who was holding a small mirror in one hand and shaving his face with a razor in the other. Xu Liang walked up to the girl and slid the package across the countertop. He paid and took the receipt, and he was about to turn to leave when the shaving man lowered the mirror and Xu Liang got a look at his whole face.

It was an awfully familiar face. Xu Liang searched his memory and very quickly came upon who it was: the young, once-handsome postman. He had changed a lot. No longer did he have a mop of thick black curls. Now his pink scalp showed through scraggly and thinning locks, and his pudgy face, shiny with grease, was liver-spotted. He had dark bags under his eyes and his neck was almost as wide as his head. Xu Liang stared at the man, then a scene flashed across his mind. Years before, he had stood in a post office, off to the side, discretely watching this very same person. The scene and its characters were mostly the same, it was just that twenty-odd years separated them. Xu Liang was a different person now, his outlook transformed. He couldn't remember what had been going through his mind back then when he first set eyes on his young love rival, but he knew without any doubt that this was his moment to go over and talk with the man, for them to chat like they were old friends. But what would he say? Well, he had to introduce himself first, and this would take some careful work; he had to make sure the guy knew that no enmity lingered, he had to convince him of his good intentions. And if that went well, Xu Liang could ask him how things were. Though, he could have guessed himself. It was obvious that things weren't great for the guy, sitting like he was at his age behind the same counter as his young colleague, and in such a new branch far out in the city's suburbs. But if his situation really was so dire, maybe Xu Liang was well-placed to help the guy out. That was perhaps what they could talk about – how he could get him moved to a better post, for example, or a better company, Xu Liang had that sort of clout now. Maybe he could get him a big pay rise. And maybe, if the conversation went well, Xu Liang would mention his first wife. He could gauge then if there was any need to go on talking about her, in a calm and collected and purely objective way, of course, like they were discussing an old acquaintance. It was through her that the two men's lives had become intertwined, after all. But he would leave all of this up to the postman, he decided. They would talk only if the guy wanted to, otherwise he wouldn't bother. Xu Liang didn't mind. He only wanted to chat. To have a friendly, casual conversation. No objective, no emotion even. And if the conversation flowed, if the men got along, then Xu Liang would see whether the guy fancied talking more, about deeper topics maybe, like life.

As Xu Liang went over to the marble counter, his nerves got to him and he hesitated. The man was still squinting at himself in the mirror and really focusing on getting all the stubble under his chin. He looked like he was enjoying himself. He was shaving very slowly, very carefully. He was moving the razor one way and then the other over a single spot, then feeling with his hand where he had just shaved. Why isn't he using an electric razor? Xu Liang wondered.

"Hello, sir," said Xu Liang.

The man looked up and glanced over Xu Liang,

stopping shaving. Then he jutted out his substantial chin and tipped his head back slightly.

"Clean?" he said

"What?" Xu Liang didn't catch his meaning.

"Did I miss anywhere?"

Xu Liang paused. "No, no. You're good."

"Well, there we go." He put down the razor. "What can I help you with?"

"Ah, erm, nothing. Never mind. I thought you were someone else," Xu Liang mumbled, turning to go.

Drinks

There was a time not long ago when I couldn't work out what had got into Lao Bu. When we all would meet up and everyone was half-cut, he chose this as the moment to float the dumbest question I could imagine: "What is love?"

Didn't I tell you?

He was slurring as he spoke, looking to each of us around the table. "No, come on, tell me. You lot, hey. Tell me. What *is* love?" He always looked like he was expecting some profound insight in response.

"Lao Bu, what is it?" friends asked. "Something up at home? Problems with the missus?"

"No, no, no," he said. "Me and the wife are fine. That's not what I mean."

The rest of us didn't really believe it was that, either.

Lao Bu was a late bloomer. He was forty before he got his act together, and he only found himself a wife a few years back. The lovebirds couldn't possibly be sick of each other yet, could they? He did have girlfriends as a younger man, was even with one for a good number of years, but they seldom lasted. The thing is Lao Bu looks like a bit of a yobbo — rough around the edges, dresses like a slob and loves a drink or ten. But he is a sensitive soul, and is a better-than-average judge of women.

What I mean by that is, if they were at all ambitious or materialistic, aching to get rich, or if they had a temper or acted spoiled or had their hearts set on a wedding dress or the red carpet, then he wasn't interested. And it worked out. Li Rong, his wife, is great. We all really like her. She's five or so years younger than him, and not pretty per se, but she suited Lao Bu just fine – and with some to spare. She dressed decent, didn't say much. One look at her and it was obvious she was an understanding person with her feet on the ground. Two years ago, before they had their daughter, Lao Bu sometimes brought Li Rong out drinking with him. She would sit at the table while the rest of us were pissed and rowdy, and she never bristled or looked uncomfortable. At most she turned to quietly suggest that Lao Bu slow down, not that he ever listened. At the end of the night when Lao Bu was sloshed, she would slip off to pay, then half-carry her wobbling husband home.

"What do you mean, then?" we asked him.

"Nothing much. Just felt like asking."

"Come on, enough now. What's wrong?"

"You can tell us if something's up, Lao Bu mate. Don't torture us with these bullshit questions."

"Forget it, then. Forget I ever asked," he said, shaking his head. He looked let down.

But we were only a few drinks in at the next meetup before he raised the topic again. "Come on, everybody, what's love?"

But after he brought this young woman to drinks, he never asked that dumb question again. We stopped wondering why he'd been asking it too.

She was an interesting girl. As carefree as they come, and not shy in the slightest. Zhan Ying was her name. She was in her twenties, slender, sexy, all delicate features and fair skin, cute as a button, really, but she drank and smoked like the rest of us and swore like a sailor when she did, "dickhead" this and "fuck" that. It took some getting used to at first, but when the mouth speaking was so pretty, were any of us going to complain?

"Fucking get this," she said one night she joined us. "Some melon head at this fast food place asked your favourite dickhead over here for her phone number yesterday. He was looking for a slap."

"Do you not know why?"

"Well, that's for me to worry about. It's got fuck-all to do with that baldie."

She fitted right in. She wasn't only as loud as the rest of us, but she loved a drinking game just as much. She knew the rules and every one of the calls for *huaquan*. Plus, she made it known how pleased she was that Lao Bu had brought her into his circle. She said it herself: she was Lao Bu's girl. And that being so, Lao Bu's friends were her friends. We were way past formalities.

When Lao Bu went to the toilet that first night, one of the group followed him and reported back afterwards.

"Look at you, mate!" he said to Lao Bu at the urinals. "Got some game, haven't you? Where did you find yourself a fine lady like that?"

"Fine?" Lao Bu said, undoing his flies. He blinked like he was trying to see it. "Yeah, I suppose she's all right, isn't she?"

"What's she do?"

"Dance teacher at an arts school."

"How long's it been?"

"Better part of a year."

"Just for fun, or is this the real deal?"

"What do you want me to say to that?"

"Are there feelings?"

Lao Bu clicked his tongue and inhaled sharply. "Well... there's, yes, there's..." He didn't seem sure. "There's something there, yes, mate... a little something."

"I should think so. Where've you ever seen a girl like that before? You've got to make a proper go of it now you've bagged one."

Lao Bu sniggered, like he was agreeing.

"The missus know?"

"Don't know. How could I let her?"

"What's the plan? Just hide it?"

Lao Bu gave a long sigh. Our friend had put his finger on the problem. "How should I know? Things are good as they are."

That night, Lao Bu and Zhan Ying left early. Zhan Ying had got carried away. She was cheers-ing anyone and everyone who asked, downing drinks left right and centre. It must have hit her hard because she threw up. She didn't want to leave, though. She was ready to keep drinking, she said. But Lao Bu said no, which ended with him dragging her up and out. One of the group saw them to the curb and helped thumb a taxi.

When the friend came back, he told us that the moment they were in the car the pair were all over each other, snogging. He cocked his head to one side and made to ape Lao Bu.

That cracked us up. We spent the rest of the night exchanging theories about what would come next. The consensus was that Lao Bu had lucked out, but it was going to land him in real hot water. A great wife at home, a daughter who'd just turned one. Divorce wouldn't exactly be an easy route, would it? And if he went for it and married Zhan Ying, who was to say how it would go? Slice it any which way and that girl still didn't look like wife material. It's all well and good to be able to drink and have fun, but marriage is much more than that.

Would he have to cut things off, and soon? One look at the twinkle in his eye and it was obvious he wouldn't. But who would, in his position? And was Zhan Ying on the same page about keeping things casual? To borrow her words, "The fuck gives that old shit the right?" What was she after, anyway? That was what we didn't know. Lao Bu could never be a sugar daddy, and he's not exactly irresistible. Basically, he had to sort this out quickly or trouble would come his way.

About damn right, too. I mean, fucking hell, a guy can't get so lucky and escape scot-free. Where would be the justice in that?

We were all pretty riled up by this conclusion, so we ordered another round of drinks and food to keep the merrymaking going. One of the guys, a divorced friend, lairy from the booze and all excited by Lao Bu's affair, started to dredge up his own tales of infidelity: "Last year I often ate at this place on the corner of Ruijin Road. There was a waitress there who was proper up for it. She would always strike up a conversation with me even if it was rammed. Then one time, I brought back a bracelet for her from a trip, made of plastic or glass, nothing special. Two *kuai* is all it cost. She was over the moon, and that night I bedded her. After that, we'd meet up whenever I had a free hour. Then there was this one afternoon, we're strolling down the street together and she starts panicking. 'Don't turn around,' she says, 'don't turn around whatever you do, my husband's behind us.' Now I didn't say a word, I just legged it. Didn't stop until I was two streets away, bent double, trying to catch my breath. I changed my number the day after, and I haven't eaten there since."

"I bet you almost broke the world hundred-metre sprint record."

"It was that or be stabbed. And that would have been no joke."

* * *

Then on the morning of Mid-Autumn Day, Lao Bu told Li Rong he had to go to work. He'd be back in time for dinner, he said. It was the holidays, and a family has to eat together for the holidays. But Lao Bu wasn't going in to work at all. He and Zhan Ying had plans in the east of the city. He still made it back for dinnertime, like he said he would, and started going on about how busy he had been the moment he stepped in the door. He was rushed off his feet, he said, all so he could make it home.

He was yammering away when he noticed that something seemed off. Why was it so quiet? "Where's the little one?" he asked Li Rong.

"I asked the babysitter to take her to my parents for the evening," she said.

This took Lao Bu by surprise. "Why's that?"

"I can't remember the last time we spent an evening together, just the two of us. It's the holiday. I'd like a quiet night in, a few drinks. Is that OK with you?"

"Of course. Of course it is."

Lao Bu felt a pang of guilt. He wondered whether, as careful as he'd been, there were places where he might have slipped up. Had he been neglecting Li Rong? Why else would she want to use the festival as a chance to reacquaint themselves? Women love their little stunts like this, it's cute but pitiful. They really do think they can change things this way. It doesn't work.

"What still needs doing? Anything I can help with?" he said, trying to sound excited.

"Nothing. The food's all ready. I only have to fry some peanuts. Actually, can you move the table and chairs onto the balcony, please? We're dining al fresco tonight."

"Of course."

Lao Bu set the tables and chairs on the balcony and opened the window. The moon was high and round in the cobalt sky. Li Rong brought out the food two dishes at a time. She had prepared a feast, and soon the table was filled with plates and bowls of different sizes, including two that contained Lao Bu's favourites, lion's head meatballs and braised eel slices.

She had gone all out. Husband and wife sat across from each other and tucked in. Li Rong topped up Lao Bu's glass when it was low, and drank more herself than she had done in the past. Her cheeks flushed red.

To do his bit for the atmosphere, Lao Bu reached over and caressed her warm-to-the-touch cheek. When he went to move his hand away, Li Rong held and pressed it against her skin for a moment longer. She had not been so affectionate in recent memory.

Li Rong raised her glass and touched it to Lao Bu's. But she didn't take a drink. She placed the glass back down and looked up at the moon. "I've got something to tell you," she said.

"Go ahead," Lao Bu said, tipping the contents of his glass down his throat.

"Don't blame me, OK?" she said quietly.

Lao Bu was taken off guard. "Blame you for what?" He eyed her expression.

"Don't blame me," she repeated.

"I won't, I won't blame you."

"You don't blame me," she said again, tears filling her eyes.

"OK, I won't blame you."

"Promise you won't." She sounded ready to break into sobs.

"Really, it's OK."

Li Rong started to cry. Lao Bu went inside and fetched some tissue for dabbing her cheeks.

Calming down somewhat, she started to talk in fits and starts. She had a lover, a colleague. She had been twisted up about the whole thing since it started, and it had caused her so much stress. The guilt she felt for what she was doing to Lao Bu, and to their daughter, kept her up at night. If she managed even only a few hours' sleep, the nightmares were constant, and she'd spent the next day in a haze, which led to mistake after mistake at work. Recently, she had also noticed her period was irregular, coming sometimes, but others not, and when it did, barely. She hadn't thought anything of it at first, because she'd never had a problem before, but then it had never been so late. She thought it was maybe to do with her mood and stress levels and the lack of sleep. A few days before, though, work had arranged physical examinations for employees and she had been told she was pregnant. She was three months along, already. The news left her numb. Even now she still felt frazzled by it. But she knew no matter what that she had to go for an abortion right away. She had contacted the clinic and booked the procedure and she was going in tomorrow. But it had come to this and she couldn't bear to hide it from Lao Bu any longer. And probably, she couldn't have, anyway, since she and Lao Bu were always safe, Lao Bu always made sure of it, so when she went to the hospital for the abortion, if she'd let anything slip and Lao Bu had found out, then he would have known what had happened, for sure. She only hoped that Lao Bu would think of their daughter and find it in himself to forgive her.

Done speaking, she burst into tears. Lao Bu sat watching her, saying nothing. A few minutes later, when he had come around from the initial shock, he listened to the sound of her crying and felt moved. Although he didn't say it in that moment, he had forgiven her already. He surprised himself with how easily the forgiveness came.

Maybe he is a just kind man at heart, who couldn't stand seeing Li Rong in such pain. A single day of a partner's love is worth a hundred days' grace, after all. Or maybe what he was really thinking about was his own stray behaviour, how his wife had only made the same mistake he had, and how he would be a hypocrite if he reacted any other way. Or maybe, under the big, round moon, with a fresh breeze blowing, one idyllic night of romance had cleansed Lao Bu of his pettiness and made a noble man of him. Or maybe, just maybe, it had occurred to Lao Bu that since he had Zhan Ying and his wife had taken a lover, wouldn't it be best if husband

and wife shake hands and be done with it, go their separate ways? Would that be so bad? Either way, the effects of the alcohol couldn't be underestimated, and it would be nothing new for a pisshead to do something they later regretted. So Lao Bu forgave Li Rong, and if the story had stopped there, a person might have been forgiven for thinking that this would see an end to Lao Bu's problems. He was a husband who could take humiliation, a generous, open-minded man. So what a shame it is that he didn't keep his mouth shut. In a rush of blood to the head, he laid the whole affair between him and Zhan Ying out on the table. It would prove to be a big mistake.

"Come on, don't cry," Lao Bu said gently. "I forgive you. Really. What if I told you something that I think will help?"

Li Rong breathed deeply until her sobbing had stopped, then wiped her tears and waited for Lao Bu to begin.

He went on to explain everything, stopping only to pick up his glass now and then for a swig. This gave his narration a rhythm that made the key details stand out extra clearly.

When he finished, he never expected Li Rong to throw her drink in his face before he had taken a breath.

"Are you mad, woman?" He jumped out of his seat.

"You dirty old perv." Li Rong swiped the dishes from the table and sent them crashing to the floor.

Peanuts scattered everywhere, and two lion's head meatballs went rolling after them. Mouth-watering chunks of braised eel flew into the air and plopped like dog shit into the wine and other dishes. Lao Bu looked on wide-eyed, his jaw swinging.

Here was a tiny issue, but what had Lao Bu expected? Had he thought he would confess his sins and the pair, freed from the weight on their shoulders and feeling reborn, would wrap each other in their arms and weep together? And when they had cried all they needed to, smiled at one another and wiped away their tears, then continued to celebrate and toast their love in the moonlight? That they would turn to planning their future? And whether that would be letting bygones be bygones and returning to happy times or splitting up so they could each have their own lives, at least they could be grateful, because things come and go, and all of it is worth cherishing.

Here were shining examples of humanity, the kind that made the world a better place. Is that what he thought would happen?

What actually happened was that Li Rong stood there among smashed plates and spilt food, snot and tears smeared across her face. "I already ended it!" she screamed at Lao Bu. "You better end it with that bitch whore too. Else I'll take our daughter and jump! I'll do it!"

"It's over, ended," Lao Bu stuttered back. "I'll break it off." At this point, he knew there was nothing for it but to call off the fling. He couldn't gamble with two lives, especially when one was a child, *his* child. What if she actually did jump? But what he couldn't wrap his head around, at that very moment, was that if *he* had done wrong, wasn't she also guilty? Didn't she also have an affair, wasn't *she* pregnant even? It was a mystery to him how she could so confidently act like justice was on her side when it felt painfully apparent that she should also feel, at least, a little bad.

"Don't... let's not get carried away. I swear I'll end it, it's already over, I promise. But one... well, you... haven't you... didn't you make a mistake too? It's not just me."

"Shut up. It's not the same. How could it be?"

"Well, why not?"

"Your piece on the side, it's dirty, shameless. You've no respect. I feel like I don't know you any more."

She was too angry to continue speaking. As far as she was concerned, for Lao Bu to have spoken in that manner was not only an insult to her feelings, it was also a smear on her character. Her face went sheet white, and she fainted. Lao Bu was terrified. She was still pregnant, what if there was some complication? He scrambled to the floor and took her in his arms.

* * *

We have all heard this tale since. Now, whenever we meet up for drinks, it's with a melancholic look on his face that a half-drunk Lao Bu has turned to the group and asked, "Hey, you lot, tell me this. Why, when they do it, is it an act of love, but when it's us, it's just fooling around, being an idiot? Yeah, tell me this, why is it love for them and being a dick when it's us?"

"You're too honest, pal."

"Victim of your own ignorance."

"That's just life. Brutal. What can you do?"

Lao Bu snorted with laughter. "Don't you all think I'm a bit of a chatty Xiang Linsao, eh? Probably, eh? From now on, call me Sharing Xiang-Lin."

Hope

I've been buying lottery tickets lately, every chance I get. Yes, for the big payout, the easy money, because who doesn't want that? But also, mostly, I do it to inject some hope into my life. My days were stuck on repeat before, same old routine, same old faces, same old thoughts, no sense that any of it was about to change. All it was good for was boring me to tears. But since I started playing the numbers, my days have got their sheen back. I'm still spending my time the same, I just have a skip in my step that wasn't there before, I have draw day to look forward to, some little hope – and it is little – that I might just win the jackpot. It's changed everything. Life is full of colour again.

Picture this. I'm strolling along and I pass by some fancy schmancy residential complex, which before I would have paid no attention to, but now, rather than not even glance that way, I stop and look, and I stand there imagining what it would be like to call that place home. Or a high-end car cruises by, and whereas before I'd have looked down or away, now I'll entertain the thought that I could be the one in the driver's seat. On the big day, I plop myself down in front of the telly, nice and early, sit through all the drawn-out run-up just so I can catch when the balls start to bounce around in the tombola then drop out one by one, and as the prizewinning combination blinks up on screen I scribble down each number and check them against my ticket. Once, twice, then one more time for good luck. I make absolutely certain I haven't missed something and, of course, I haven't, and I haven't won anything either, or else I wouldn't be writing this article for peanuts. But it's nothing to stress about, there is always next time. There's always that hope.

Most weeks I buy five tickets, all at once. Ten yuan altogether. I don't splash out any more than that, I can't, my pockets have bottoms. But also, when it comes to winning, it doesn't matter how many or how few times you play. The papers are full of stories that prove it. A vegetable farmer buys two on his way to market and wins. Some retired geezer buys three and snaps up the big prize on his first time playing. A business owner, five hundred grand in debt, desperate, buys ten, wins five mil. You can't argue with evidence like that.

I've also picked up a couple of tricks from the papers. For starters, you have to act like buying the tickets is no big thing. It's best to make the purchase on a whim and forget about it as soon as you're done. Then, when the draw comes around, you conveniently remember, Ah, look what I bought. You check your numbers, all casual like, and bingo, you've won. That's how I do it, anyway.

The vendor is up ahead, I've spotted it from down the street, the urge kicks in – this is precisely when I exercise self-restraint. The only situation allowed is where I wander by, minding my own business, and just before the stall vanishes over my shoulder I turn and go in, buy five tickets before I've even had the chance to stop myself. And straight afterwards it's forgotten. I don't think about the lottery again until I've flicked to the channel on the day, you know, not really trying to find it, and I've got nothing else on, so how about I just have a quick check... Not a single match. Typical.

But I've got plenty more tricks where that came from. Just please excuse me for not giving them all away for free here. We all have to be a little selfish sometimes, don't we? Plus, I have a feeling my lucky day isn't far off now. At least, that's what I hope.

I'll Tell You a Secret

It was already past eight when we left Zhu Jun's place, and we only got as far as Xiyuan Street before we started dithering over where to go. The plan before we stepped out of the door was to find some girls to chat with at East University. Back in Zhu Jun's bright living room, it had sounded like an attractive idea. But standing on a street corner in the dark, it quickly dawned on us all that the plan was ridiculous: who would we even talk to? We didn't know a single female student there between us. How we hadn't thought of that back at Zhu Jun's was anybody's guess. But the reasonable explanation is not that we hadn't, but that our concern for a more impending problem had won out: four men lolling around together is about as boring as it gets.

We had gone around for more than that, obviously,

we had a happy night of cards in mind. But the game we usually played is called "Finding Friends" and needs six players, and Liu Ligan and Old Huang never showed. We had to find some different entertainment.

East Uni was just around the corner, and the girls there were famously open-minded.

"Let's go to the uni," said Old Hu. "We can stroll around the campus, and if we see anyone we like the look of we go over and chat."

"So you'll go over first?" asked Tao Nan. Old Hu went quiet. He was right to, we were all past the age when we could strike up conversations with strange girls and risk taking a few insults on the chin but still come away unscathed.

We were as good as middle-aged and just starting to make something of ourselves, we couldn't afford to be labelled as scoundrels because of a little trouble.

"Why not go to Huang's?" said Zhu Jun. Old Huang lived close by, in Xuanwumen, but what would we do there? The fact he'd said he was joining us and then hadn't probably meant he'd had a row with the wife. It was no secret that the couple were always fighting, mostly because Old Huang had been caught once again looking for greener grass or his wife's most recent affair had given him leverage. They weren't the best-behaved couple, and were a jealous pair at that, so not a week went by when they weren't at each other's throats.

But somehow, of all of us, it was only this clown and his wife who were still together and in love. Turns out that a happy marriage requires lubrication. It's a shame that by the time we cottoned on to this fact, it was already too late.

"How about a bar?" said Tao Nan.

"I don't mind. Up to you?" said Zhu Jun, looking at me and Old Hu.

"I reckon we call it a night," I suggested. I preferred saying goodbye and getting to do something proper with my evening over pickling ourselves in a bar.

Moreover, I couldn't decide if it was too late already to call the young woman I was seeing, ask if she wanted to meet at mine. Spending time with her wasn't all that interesting if I'm honest, and it came with its risks, but the night didn't promise much else. Recently, when we'd been together, she kept asking if she could stay at mine should she ever fall out with her mum. I was especially careful with how I answered: "Of course you can stay here, but I wouldn't want you arguing with your mum over me. The only people who will ever really love you are your parents. A lover's love can't compare. You'll see it someday."

It was a shame she didn't already. "You're only saying that because you're scared I'll get hung up on you."

She wasn't wrong, but I couldn't admit it. "That's not what I mean."

"Yes, it is."

There was nothing else to do at this point but to have sex. Luckily, I still had the capacity. "You're so cute when you're angry," I'd say as I pulled her into my arms.

I was well aware the relationship wouldn't last, but this only made me desire her more.

"You guys have fun," I said, seeing they weren't responding to my suggestion. "I'm off."

"Come on, stay out," said Old Hu, tugging my arm. He was recently divorced and at the stage when loneliness becomes too much to bear. He was desperate for solace among friends.

Poor guy.

"You've got a woman waiting for you," said Zhu Jun, obviously disappointed. "You put sex before mates."

"I'm knackered," I said, trying to sound regretful while looking drawn. "Work's been busy." I gave them a wave and headed to the nearest bus stop.

And when I left, something happened. Something that, were it to get out, they said, threatened to ruin the three guys' reputations. What exactly that could be in this day and age, I struggled to imagine.

* * *

I was at home reading that Sunday afternoon when Zhu Jun called. He asked me what I was up to and did I fancy going over to a girl's? What type of girl? I asked. The host of the radio show *Literary Stars*. He made it clear that she had been the one to ask him round. So it was him she wanted there, not me, I said, why would I go?

"The problem is," he said, "she has friends over. I guess a bunch of women. So I told her I'd bring a friend. Interested?"

He had my attention. We arranged that he would come to mine and we'd get a taxi together. Twenty minutes later, he turned up with a black leather bucket bag on his back and made me wait while he changed into a green jacket. We waved down a taxi outside and climbed in. "Emei Ridge," he told the driver.

"Emei Ridge?" I said. "Where's that, why've I never heard of it?"

"There are plenty of places you've never heard of," said Zhu Jun. Then to the driver, "You know it?"

The driver nodded. The car took South Taiping Road.

"It's a brilliant name," I said in excitement. Excitement that might have had more than a little to do with the prospect of meeting those girls. "Imagine if everywhere in the city had a weird name like that. Just stepping out of the door there'd be a sense of mystique.

You ask someone where they're off to and they say Wild Boar Forest. Imagine that."

"What if we changed everyone's names too?" said Zhu Jun. "To, like, Sun Erniang, the bandit from *Water Margin*, and Tiger Li."

"It's not a bad idea," I said, chuckling. "How about other words we use every day? You go in a coffee shop and shout, 'Barkeep, your finest ale.'"

"And three pounds of dog meat, hot through and chopped, with a plate of your best human dumplings!"

"And to a hooker, 'Mistress, how much silver to keep sire company?'"

"Or the shopkeeper's wife, 'Lady-love, who's that rogue behind the counter there? Your lord? Has he got his shifty eyes on sire's bundle?'"

The driver gave us a look in the rear-view mirror and I shot him a smirk. Shortly after crossing Xinjiekou, he turned into an alley. "A bit further. Almost there," said Zhu Jun, pointing ahead. "Here. Here we are."

Getting out, we discovered that "Emei Ridge" was little more than a tall slope, between Xinjiekou and Hanzhongmen, with tall buildings on all sides and, among them, the odd bungalow that hadn't yet been torn down. It was a residential area. One that had been there for some years already by the look of the building facades and oversized balconies and drainpipes spotted with rust. Emei Ridge must have been a historical name,

I thought to myself. Centuries earlier, this might well have been a patch of wilderness on the edge of the city, roamed by wild animals and highwaymen waiting for unsuspecting travellers. On moonless, windy nights, the sound of rustling and growling would have made it a gloomy, unnerving place to be. But with time, over hundreds of years, it had changed into a different space entirely, and all that was left of its past was that misleading, eternal name.

Zhu Jun led me through a steel gate and into a building. We climbed to the first floor, where he knocked on the door next to the stairway. The sound of footsteps. The door opened.

An average-looking woman stood on the other side. She was wearing jeans and a tucked-in floral shirt, her hair was lightly permed, and she held a hand of playing cards. "Hey, Zhu Jun," she chirped. "As if you came. To what do I owe the pleasure?"

We followed her inside. The living room was an unusual shape. Part of the wall jutted into the room with a curtain across its face, and visible through the gap in the middle was a space with a refrigerator, wardrobe and a bed.

There were also two doors on one side of the living room, one locked and the other open, and on the other side, the kitchen and bathroom. "This is my friend, Lu Chunguang," Zhu Jun said to the woman. "He's the editor of *Literary Wave* magazine." Then to me, "This is Xu Xiaojie."

"Come on through," said Xu Xiaojie, heading towards the open door. We went in after her and I felt a chill run through me, as if I'd taken a bucket of cold water full to the face. The girl I had been imagining – the same one that Zhu Jun had promised – was nowhere to be seen. Instead, three young lads were sitting around a table in the room's centre, each with a hand of cards.

"This is Zhu Jun, my favourite young writer," Xu announced to the three men. "And this is... Lu... Lu..."

"Lu Chunguang," I said weakly.

"*Literary Wave*'s editor," Zhu Jun chipped in, as if to save me from ridicule.

"These are my colleagues at the radio station." Xu introduced each of them and the show they managed, but I had no idea who was who. They could have been Wang Two, Zhang Three and Li Four as far as I cared. The lads gave us a cold hello, tossed their cards into the middle of the table and said nothing more.

Zhu Jun opened his bucket bag and fished out a book which he gave to Xu Xiaojie.

"This is my newest story collection," he said. "It's for you."

Xu took the book and looked at the cover. "Have you signed it?" she asked. When she got the yes she wanted, she put the book down on the table between the men. "Look at this book by my favourite writer."

"We're not readers," said one of the men.

"Unless it's a comic," said another.

What did they mean by that? Was this prickliness towards me and Zhu Jun or were they joking around? Either way, the atmosphere was awkward. Not that I minded. I like to bask in a little misfortune every now and then. We weren't there for me, anyway, and the reason I was there – cute, bubbly girls – had lumped me in a room full of numbskull men. Disappointed didn't cut it.

So I was in no mood to worry about awkwardness, and it wasn't on me to try to cheer everyone up. I plopped myself down on the single bed against the wall and grabbed from next to the pillow a magazine with a colourful cover.

"You can sit down," said Xu Xiaojie dragging over a chair for Zhu Jun before sitting on the other single bed herself. She seemed oblivious to the atmosphere, but she could just as well have been secretly enjoying it, I couldn't say. It's this sort of situation where womanly craftiness and vanity come into play. Nothing in her expression said she was uncomfortable, anyway. "Are you working on anything big at the moment?" she asked Zhu Jun.

"More short stories," he said. "Lü Mei?"

"She's out. She has a boyfriend now."

"Aren't there another couple of women living here too?"

"They're away on a work trip, doing interviews. Are you disappointed?"

"Come on, now, I'm happy to see you."

"That's a lie."

One of the three guys rose slightly to reach for the TV on the desk by the wall and switched it on. I glanced at the three of them. Their expressions, watching the screen, were pure concentration, like the cartoon that was on was something special. It occurred to me then that maybe they were having the exact same experience as I was. Xu Xiaojie could have invited them over with some vague suggestion that two other friends were also coming, which they naturally assumed meant two girls. Ideal: three men, three women, it would be like a blind date. Then before they know it Zhu Jun and I have barged in. There now being five men and one woman, it had put a damper on things. Had I asked them, it was probably Zhu Jun and I who owed the three an apology, as men. But they could just as well have said sorry to us.

Then again, if there really had been five women there, it ought to have been us doing the apologising, to Xu Xiaojie.

But she clearly didn't like her own sex, or else why

did she choose to spend a rare Sunday with so many men?

I chuckled to myself at the thought, and it helped lift my mood a little. I turned my attention back to the magazine in my lap and started flicking through. Zhu Jun and Xu Xiaojie were still half-flirting off to the side. They were onto which girl from the flat was Zhu Jun's favourite – turns out he was a regular guest – and Xu was determined to prove that it was the one called He Bingling, and that he was only using Lü Mei to get to her. Zhu Jun vehemently denied everything. He was fond of someone though, he said, none other than Xu Xiaojie herself. A laugh that could have been a cough came from one of the three lads. I couldn't tell if it was in response to something Zhu Jun and Xu had said, or something on the telly.

I stopped on an interesting piece in the magazine. A Dutch women's football player had decided her hefty chest was hindering her performance and had gone for a breast reduction. After the surgery, with her new washboard chest, she was suddenly able to gain a few extra yards on her opponents, and she became a first-rate striker. But this brought with it some controversy, with some people quite rightly pointing out that if this was allowed, then as women's football grew in popularity and funding, there was a chance that a lot more players would make the same decision, and the pitch would become a battlefield of flat-chests, and in that case, was it really still women's football? They would just be men without cocks.

I had to laugh. "What're you giggling at?" Zhu Jun asked over his shoulder.

"Nothing."

"Stop reading that." He leaned over and swiped the magazine, throwing it aside. "Chat with us instead."

About what? I thought. What could I contribute? I leant back with my palms face up on the bed and surveyed the room.

There was a fridge next to each single bed. So the girls who slept there weren't close, otherwise one for the room should have been enough. Each side also had a chest of drawers and a desk, but there was only one TV. Clearly the girls' financial situations differed enough that they couldn't have the same of everything. There were also modern paintings in gold frames hung on the walls next to some weird-shaped decorations that had no obvious attachments keeping them there.

The light in the room was fading. Xu Xiaojie stood up to switch on a lamp. "Everyone hungry?" she said. "I'll make something."

"Not for us," one of the three guys replied. "We're going in a sec."

"Where? Eat here."

"No thanks, we've got plans."

I thought at that point Xu would let it go and shoo the three plague bearers out. But she stood her ground. "Nonsense. You didn't tell me that when you got here. Eat and then go."

Since they weren't leaving, it was time for us to make a move. I gave Zhu Jun a look.

"Xu Xiaojie," he said. "You're busy, we'll go."

"What is wrong with you lot?" She sounded genuinely annoyed. "I've bought in food but you all want to leave. Are you trying to piss me off?"

That was the last thing we wanted to do.

* * *

The something she was going to make turned out to be a feast. She cooked lots of different dishes and, as if by magic, made eight bottles of beer appear out of nowhere. She kept raising her glass and toasting us as we ate, but the atmosphere barely changed. The three guys chatted among themselves, and Zhu Jun and I did the same, with Xu flitting between our conversations and reminding us to eat. But she didn't seem bothered, she was like a fish in water, and a jolly one at that.

After eating, we said our goodbyes first. It was already dark when we stepped outside, my face welcoming the breeze, flushed and hot from the alcohol as it was. I thought I could smell the pleasing, cool damp of mountain air. We descended the gently sloping alley that was Emei Ridge, passing under the sparse streetlamps and through the patches of dark. But I knew no tiger was going to jump out.

"I walked right into your trap," I said.

"I'm as confused as you are," said Zhu Jun. "I can't say what her goal was calling me round."

I thought about this. It was a genuine question. "Maybe she called you to upset those guys," I said, "or she called them to provoke you. Or so you could all annoy each other. If that's the case, she was sorely mistaken."

"I won't go there again. Besides, that girl is too in-your-face, she wouldn't make a good lover. Lü Mei is different. But they all think too highly of themselves. They're smart girls but they each have their hearts set on some great love. There's no such thing as casual flirting or a little date with them, it has to be serious."

We were out of the alley and onto the street by now. "Got any plans this evening?" asked Zhu Jun. I hadn't. "Let's go to yours, then," he said. "We can walk, we've nothing else to do."

We set off in the direction of Xinjiekou. Neither of us said anything for a while. Zhu Jun looked to be thinking about something, and I was peering through coffee shop windows at the interiors made hazy by the glare from streetlamps, making up stories about the relationships of all the couples inside.

"I'll tell you a secret," said Zhu Jun suddenly.

"What's that?" I spun my head his way, a little surprised.

"I shouldn't be telling you at all, to be honest. It will be the end of us if it gets out," he said, fixing me with a grave look.

I figured he was hamming up the potential risk just so I'd regard his telling me as fair compensation for letting me down earlier on. Still, he had my curiosity. Because what could be so bad as that? "Relax, all right," I said. "I won't tell a soul."

"But..." There was hesitation in his face.

"I vow that it won't pass my lips," I said. "Won't that do?"

"OK, OK." He had decided. "Do you remember a fortnight ago, when you came to mine for cards? When Liu Ligan and Old Huang abandoned us so we ended up wandering around aimlessly."

I nodded.

* * *

So after you had gone, he continued, the three of us stood around on the crossroads for a few minutes trying to decide whether to call it a day like you had, or find somewhere fun to go. We settled on Urban Cowboy, the bar. It was still early and we fancied a beer.

We took a taxi. The bar is next to Zhonglou Park, I imagine you've not been. The décor is something special. Wood walls made to look like exposed brick, and adorned with all of these metallic things, a bull's head, a saddle, cowboy boots, a revolver, a double-barrelled shotgun, a poster of a Western shootout. Next to the bar on a wooden frame there was a great big barrel laid on its side. The bunker lights dangling from the ceiling were all rusted and the dim lighting made the room look smoky. It was pretty empty when we went in, just some foreigners – two guys and a girl – playing pool with a Chinese girl and, on the other side, two girls playing darts. One of them was very curvy. Every time she threw a dart, her tits would jiggle. There were people upstairs as well, on the mezzanine over the bar, who we could just about hear talking. We found a table and ordered some small Tsingtao beers which we drank from the bottle.

"Hey," said Tao Nan, who jutted his chin in the direction of the pool table, "that girl over there and the three foreigners don't look like they're together."

I turned to look. Tao Nan was right. The three foreigners were yapping away between shots while the girl stood off to one side looking sorry for herself and staring expressionless at the pool table. It was only on her turn that she perked up, flicking her hair aside and bending over the table, expertly holding the cue.

Then the foreign girl was lining up a shot when she suddenly turned and pushed the Chinese one hard, probably for standing too close.

"Weird," I said.

"Maybe she's a prostitute." Old Hu threw his comment out like it meant nothing. I didn't agree. She was wearing a batik shirt and an ankle-length tube skirt with a tribal pattern. Her hair was cut to her shoulders. She looked cultured.

"I'll go and see what it's about," Tao said, standing up and making his way over.

At which, Old Hu, looking jittery all of a sudden, took two long swigs of beer and sent a look in the direction of the darts players. "I fancy some darts," he said. "You coming?"

He wasn't thinking about darts, that I knew. "You go," I said.

"Really?" he said. He looked like he was regretting the decision already. "I'll go by myself, then." He picked up his beer bottle and drank another mouthful, then loped over there like he was a bear. I sat sipping my beer, keeping an eye on them. Tao Nan was standing next to the Chinese girl and staring just like her at the pool table, saying nothing, like they were having a minute's silence.

Old Hu quickly managed to ingratiate himself into the dart players' ranks. He lined up his throw, his body leant slightly forward, raised on his tiptoes, eyes squinted. His round figure rocked from side to side as he tried to find his balance. He looked so ridiculous that the curvy girl playing with him broke into a chortle, which started her breasts bouncing. He released and his dart hit the wall about a metre from the board, as expected. How had I never seen Old Hu before as a guy who could work the ladies? We've all been fooled by his simple face.

Tao Nan, meantime, was saying something to the Chinese girl.

Something like, "Don't be sad," maybe? She ignored him, resolute in her sadness. They resumed their silent tribute, staring at the pool table.

I stayed put a moment longer, then bored, told the server not to clear the table. I stood and climbed the stairs to the mezzanine. I wanted to see what fun there was to be had. Zero, it turned out. There were only some dark seating booths already occupied by various couples wrapped around each other having themselves a good old time. When I headed back down, the situation had changed.

* * *

Zhu Jun stopped the story there. "I can't," he said, "I shouldn't tell you."

"No! Why?" He had already whet my appetite. "Go on."

"I really can't. This isn't just about me, it involves Tao Nan and Lao Hu. I can't go around spilling others' secrets."

"Fuck's sake. We're old friends. We don't have secrets."

"This is different. It's not just any secret... if people found out–"

"All right," I said, losing my patience. "I've already vowed not to tell. What else do you want?"

"It's best you don't know," he said before ignoring me once more and walking ahead. I quickened my pace and caught him by the arm.

"You've already told me the start, you can't not tell me the rest." I pinched him hard. "Out with it."

"Ouch!" he squealed, flinching and pulling his arm away. "How about this, you tell me one of your secrets first, then I'll tell you this one?"

"What secret could I even have?"

"If you can't think of one, you'll just have to forgive me for not sharing. Nowadays, we're all about fair trade, aren't we?"

"Well, give me a moment." I slowed down my

walking and tried to recall something worthwhile. "A few days ago, I fucked a girl who isn't even twenty yet–"

"All right, all right," said Zhu Jun. "What sort of secret is that? If that's what you call a secret, I've got ten I could tell you right now. Realer than that! Don't be such a crook. Trying to fob me off with pocket change to get the motherlode."

Zhu Jun was right, that was no secret. But I had nothing else to offer. "I don't have any secrets, really," I said sincerely.

"There's no rush, keep thinking." He was genuinely encouraging me. "What awful deeds are you afraid of people knowing?"

I supposed having lived to this age I must have done my fair share of sordid things, but there was nothing people couldn't know. Did people even have secrets any more? Even homosexuals were coming out into the open. Our graphic designer at work was gay and never hid his sexuality – not even with strangers. He went to gay get-togethers at night and would thumb a taxi, climb in and announce to the driver, "I'm gay." Then he'd watch for the driver's reaction, fascinated. He always made sure to take taxis driven by men, and always sat in the front passenger seat.

"That driver almost killed me with how much he made me laugh," he told us the next day in the office once. "He froze and didn't dare look at me, like a frightened virgin. A big bearded guy. Pah."

Zhu Jun patted my shoulder. "Thought of one, mate? Tell me when you have, no need to be embarrassed," he said.

"I fucked a homo," I said.

"Really?" he said. His expression read shock. "How?"

"With a metal poker."

"Was it fun?"

"The most."

"Fucking hell. Making a secret up gets you a fine by the way – two secrets. Is there really not one you can say?"

There wasn't, truly. Not one. I thought of myself as a pretty pitiful guy then – not one decent secret, but I figured it was the same for most of our generation, that it would be a struggle to come up with something. This was part of the reason I was so eager to hear Zhu Jun's. I was hungry for a truly good secret. The previous generation and us are different in that way. No doubt they lived in a time that was full of secrets. I say that with my dad in mind. It was thanks to his parents hiding a secret that he'd been able to lead a happy life for so long. I say "until now" because my mum was sick and didn't seem to have long left, and Dad was faced with the prospect of living alone after her death, so there was a chance his happy life would also be coming to an end soon...

He had been a soldier as a young man, which back then meant he took part in the Revolution, and after victory, though he was still young for the role and uneducated, he soon went from officer to regiment commander. But the bigger stroke of luck was that after so many years serving the Motherland and the People with no time to think of his own happiness, and even though he was long past the usual age for marriage, the administration saw what he needed and decided to look after its good comrade, so he was introduced to a number of politically watertight women. But each of them was rejected, outright, by my almost illiterate and ageing father. He might not have been able to read a book, but he could read a woman's face, no problem. Then one Spring Festival, a local song-and-dance troupe arrived to put on a performance for his regiment as thanks for its service, and straight away the vocal soloist for *The Bright Sky in the Liberated Areas* caught his eye. The commander, seeing it his duty to aid his men, stepped in personally to tell the singer, "Comrade Lu is the best cadre in my army. Born into farming stock, he has worked hard all his life and suffered for it, displaying unwavering loyalty to the Party and the People. He showed courage on the battlefield and didn't shrink from real action. He is a team worker... To couple with such an exemplary comrade and become partners in arms should be any girl's ultimate happiness." The singer hesitated at first, she was a student after all and was hoping to find someone educated, and he had never been the most handsome man... But the commander's continued efforts to persuade her eventually won out, and she agreed to become Comrade Lu's revolutionary partner.

Before they married, my mum went out in public with my dad just once. She had seen what the regiment received for rations and was afraid he would be in need of a good meal, so she brought along some cans of meat only to have him thunder at her on seeing them. "You've more money than sense, why waste it on this luxury rubbish?"

Once they tied the knot and my mum had started to pop out children, she discovered, by stealing a glance at a letter from my dad's hometown, that he had already married before signing up, and he had two kids.

Years later Mum would tell me, "If I'd known he had a wife I wouldn't have agreed to marry him, whatever his circumstances." But Dad did right, otherwise this fucking world wouldn't have me in it.

Thinking of Dad's secret reminded me of the one my mum had been guarding all her life. Whether she was ever as happy in their marriage as Dad? I realised it was quite possible I would never find out. I wasn't going to stand over my dying mother's bed to ask, "How has your life been? Happy?" Let her have her secret, I thought, it might end up being the one thing she can take with her.

* * *

We had crossed the Xinjiekou and Daxinggong neighbourhoods and were walking down South Taiping Road. It was a bustling street; the next stretch alone boasted an Imperial Leisure Spa, an East Sea Pleasure Park and a Bang Disco. Their queer neon signs glinting against the night sky all hinted at an extraordinary time.

"You still haven't thought of one?" said Zhu Jun. "Then you can't complain."

We were almost at Baixia Junction. A left turn and we'd be at mine.

There on the corner was a Xinhua Bookshop. I stopped by the door. "Wait, I've got one," I said.

"Go on, then." Zhu Jun stopped too.

"You see that giant book in there?" I said, pointing at the bookshop.

"What giant book?" Zhu Jun asked, scanning the window display. "Where?"

"Take a few steps back, then look closely."

He did as I said, but was none the wiser. "I don't see anything."

"Look up."

Zhu Jun cocked his head and narrowed his eyes. "What do you know, there *is* a giant book up there," he said. "Weird, I've been coming to this bookshop forever and never noticed it before."

It was hard to spot, to be fair. There, under the glaring shop sign, a white model made of wood depicting an open book. It was close in colour to the cream of the shop's walls and surrounded by all these eye-catching ads and displays, so it was easily missed.

"There you go, that's a secret," I said, "and an interesting one too. Whoever designed it must have put in a lot of effort. They probably thought it was really creative and would have people singing their praises. What they never imagined was their masterpiece would end up hidden from view where no one would ever find it. There's something to that – an individual's efforts always go unnoticed, are insignificant. And another thing: if we pay close enough attention, we'll find lots in life that others don't know, and our lives will be all the more beautiful for it. Life will be worth living."

"All right," I said, finally. "I've told you a secret. Now it's your turn."

Everyone Needs a Rich Friend

Everyone needs a rich friend, even if only to treat you to dinner and a night on the town, though that's plenty for me.

Zhang Chao is mine. He hadn't had his business in Shenzhen ten years before he hit it big and bought himself a place and a car, and even married an attractive woman over there who was pretty capable herself. He comes back occasionally to tell us how well the company is doing. Apparently, he can be away and, as long as the wife is still there, then the business will keep ticking over just fine. When he has come home in the past, he has always taken us friends out for meals and drinks and sometimes to the sauna for massages and a little something extra to keep us happy. For him to strike it rich like he has and still remember us all, where he came from, that wasn't a given, and we really appreciated it. If only all moneybags were like Zhang Chao.

Last time he was back was the end of this past summer. He took us all out to dinner, as per.

He had a handheld camcorder with him and seemed obsessed with it. He strapped it to his hand when we were eating and filmed us the whole time, stopping only to show us the footage every now and then on the camera's colour screen. It was a small screen but still big enough for us to tell we were having it large, stuffing our faces and downing drinks. There was nothing more to it than that, but Zhang Chao was chuffed. He'd watch the video with us, then watch us watching it with a big grin on his face. "It's good isn't it?" he kept saying. We made out like we were blown away, but none of us really thought it was all that neat. We were just having a meal, why did we need to watch ourselves back on a screen? He filmed us at the bars afterwards, too, and when we were outside, walking together, chatting. He never put the camera down once. If he wasn't shooting us then it was a tree or building, the street we were on. Pretty much anything. What he planned to do with all that film I'd no idea. Best I can tell, the wealthy don't have the same interests as us paupers.

I spent my evenings last summer on Gulou Square. I'd call up a friend and we'd enjoy some ice-cold beers on the stone benches by the grass, talking, people-watching. It felt like everyone in the city was there, the youth in all their best gear, prostitutes, rent boys. There was a fountain in the middle of the square that lit up different colours, and parents liked to stop next to it with their kids to watch the water shoot upwards and change colour. It was a big, open space, airy and cool thanks to the nice breeze. The floor was terrazzo and the grass was lined with bollard lights that turned the green beneath them hazy with their soft lighting. We'd wait until about midnight when most people had cleared off and then summon our liquid courage to approach the prostitutes, chat them up a little and try to agree a price, which never happened because we weren't remotely sincere, it was purely for fun. But they didn't take us seriously anyway, probably on account of the flip-flops and beer bottles. We didn't exactly look like we were there to do business. So they kept our chats short, but they were still good value. Talking with them was an education. They had stripped away any hang-ups about certain topics, and nothing was out of bounds. Some of the filthiest stuff was new even to us. The rent boys, by comparison, were reserved.

One time Ding Lu and I watched this young guy stroll round in circles for ages glancing about the place. We assumed he was turning tricks, so I shouted him over when he next passed by and asked him why he was loitering. He said in an accent I couldn't place that he was supposed to meet a friend, but they hadn't shown. I told him not to talk shit, we knew what he was doing. We invited him to sit and chat, told him we were all "comrades" here and put my arm around Ding Lu's shoulders as I spoke. He sat with us, and Ding Lu offered him a beer that he didn't want but Ding Lu insisted. He couldn't drink for the life of him, though. A couple of sips and his tongue loosened up and he started jabbering on. He was from Sheng County, in Zhejiang, the home of Yue opera. His whole family were opera singers. He had been in a company himself before, but it had gone under, and so struggling to make a living he had come to the city to see what he could do. We asked him to sing us something and he threw up two orchid gestures, thumbs and forefingers touching with the other fingers raised, and started to sing. He was good, we kept telling him. We toasted him a bunch as we did and soon he was chucking up and wobbling all over the place and falling into me so I'd catch him. He hadn't even finished the bottle. After he had fallen into me a couple of times I whispered in his ear, How much for the night, and he said really softly that we only needed to say a price and he'd happily go anywhere with us. All right, I said, how about fifty, and you go with my friend there. I winked at Ding Lu, then stood up and set off walking. After a few paces, I looked back and saw Ding Lu jumping up like there was a fire under his arse and running to catch me up. We piss ourselves every time we bring it up.

What I'm trying to say is, see how much fun you can have without spending a fortune?

I asked Zhang Chao if he fancied going to the square when he was back, but he wasn't interested. "What would we even do there?" he asked. "If you want to drink, let's go to a bar."

I like a bar, don't get me wrong, but one small bottle of beer was at least fifteen *kuai*, when a big one was only three on the street, and if you took the bottle back they gave you five *mao*. That's two *kuai* five *mao* for a beer.

So one beer in a bar cost about the same as a whole night on Gulou Square. And if all we were doing was drinking and having a laugh, why not save some money? But if Zhang Chao wanted to hit the town, I wasn't going to complain. I wouldn't be getting the bill.

On one of our nights out, Zhang Chao announced that he wanted to shoot a short film, with a plot, and he already had the story all figured out. The boys thought the idea wasn't bad. It would be more interesting than him filming us eat, anyway. This explained why the camera had been recording all those random things, he had a plan all along. Then he said the film needed only two actors, and he had settled on Zhu Qiang and me. When the rest of them started grumbling that they wanted to be in it too, Zhang Chao said that if the first film went well he would do more in the future. Everyone would get their chance.

"Why two men?" asked Zhu Qiang. "You should find a woman so you can film her and the guy getting frisky. Go the whole hog. It's guaranteed entertainment."

Zhang Chao told him to calm down, there was no hurry. He would get to that in good time.

"Check this bloke," I said, looking at Zhu Qiang, "he's all talk. He wouldn't dare do a sex scene." I wasn't just saying this, either. Zhu Qiang was a mouse.

Zhu Qiang and I had been on Gulou Square again, one night not long before then. We stayed until midnight and were about to leave when we found a young woman lying under the portico of the post office at the edge of the square. Zhu Qiang said we should see what was going on. We went up and asked why she was lying there. She was sleeping, she said. She had come from the countryside to work and hadn't found a gig yet. A bed in a hostel cost, so she would make do outside. We told her it wasn't safe, you never know who might come along, and a private room was pennies, too. She couldn't sleep there, we said, she was best off finding a bed.

She didn't listen. She was set on staying there for the night. We tried persuading her some more, then gave up. After we'd walked a while, Zhu Qiang turned to me and said, "You live alone, why didn't you take the woman back to yours?"

I wasn't interested, though. "You take her if you want to," I said. But he had a wife, how could he? Looking at him, I knew this wasn't him joking around, so I made a suggestion. "Find a hostel and pay for her to stay the night, she'll be grateful beyond words and that's when you make your move. She won't say no. You can go home when you're finished."

"No way, are you mad?" he replied, a spooked look on his face. "What if the police turned up? Or she got attached?"

I broke it down for him, to stop him worrying. There was nothing dangerous about doing what I'd suggested, but still, he didn't go back. I proposed we leave it, and the two of us walked to the next crossroads where we were about to part when he asked, "You mean it? No danger?" None, I said. He nodded and stuck out an arm to wave down a taxi which he climbed into looking pensive. The next time we saw each other, he brought up that night. "You really think if we took that woman to a hostel there would have been no trouble? Really, though?" he said.

* * *

The two of us were in a taxi with Zhang Chao headed for the riverside. We had driven beyond the built-up areas of the city sprawl and were passing through a long stretch of residential buildings. When we pulled up at the dock, we got out and waited to board the ferry to Bagua Island. This was Zhang Chao's idea. All he had said over the phone was we were going to shoot a film and we wouldn't be back that evening.

He didn't even give away what the film was about or why we had to go to Bagua Island to make it. But neither did we ask. There was no need, we weren't exactly suffering. Honestly, start to spend any time with the moneyed and you notice a sense of relief coming over you, like nothing can go wrong, and it's not even just because of all the food and drink to be had, sometimes it boils down to knowing there's probably something fun and novel around the corner. Like the year before when Zhang Chao was home. He took us all out for dinner and then suggested we go singing at a karaoke hall. We were up for anything, so we ended up at this place called Impulse. Zhang Chao hired a room and ordered drinks, then asked the head waiter to bring in a selection of hostesses for us each to take our pick.

The women were gems, every one of them, properly gorgeous. We flung our arms around them and belted tunes and drank. What a time. I remember that mine was Sichuanese, she can't have been twenty yet, and so perky. She couldn't hold a tune, but she was happy to give me riddles to guess, for a drinking game. "A naked man sits on a rock," she said. "What's the idiom?" I couldn't get it.

"To strike an egg against a stone. Drink! OK, another. Two naked men are sitting on a rock." I didn't know. "To kill two birds with one stone. You're thick! Drink! Na-ah, finish it! OK, one more. A naked woman sits on a rock." I had no idea.

"*Yin xiao shi da* – to lose a lot trying to save a little. Get it? It sounds like 'little pussy, big stone'." It's safe to say I got so drunk I can't remember how I made it home.

Waiting for the ferry to come, we did a lap of the waiting room, but there were no empty seats, so we went to sit in the shade of a tree outside. It was the afternoon, and the heat was prickly. Zhang Chao bought us each a mineral water from the booth and we sipped at those and smoked. On the street that ran next to the dock were some dogs sniffing around and people playing chess in front of a shop with a huddle of onlookers. Zhang Chao flicked his cig end and said he wanted to test the lens. He asked me to head down the street, then turn around and wander back, acting natural, then stop by the chess game to lean in for a look. I asked if I could smoke and he said it was up to me. So, cig dangling from my lips, I did as he said, with him positioned several paces in front of me walking backwards and filming. Everyone on the street including the chess players and their audience looked up at us both, which made me uneasy, but it calmed me down to start puffing on the cigarette. When we were done, Zhang Chao asked Zhu Qiang to give it a go. He was picking his lead man.

The ferry arrived and we boarded with the crowd from the waiting room. Most of them were country types, I could tell from their clothes. Some were pushing bikes along, others had empty produce baskets. When we were moving, Zhang Chao stood at the railings and recorded a tugboat puttering by, before turning his lens on the Yangtze River Bridge in the distance. We reached the far dock in less than twenty minutes.

Bagua Island sits in the middle of the Yangtze and covers an area of about thirty square miles. I hadn't been in years, and the best I could remember it was all countryside. Just regular farmland and plots.

It had changed a lot since then. We left the dock onto a busy street with shops and stalls lining its length and people bustling here and there. Directly opposite the exit was this massive advertisement hoarding with a picture on it of striped pyjamas and two words in blocky font over them: Cloud Mine. Zhu Qiang gazed up at the ad. "What a great name for pyjamas," he said after a moment.

I wasn't convinced. "What's so good about that?" I asked. "It's naff."

Zhu Qiang said I didn't understand, it was imaginative.

"Imaginative my arse," I said.

"Do you know what putting on your pyjamas means?" he said. "It means sleep. And what does sleep mean? It means fucking. And what does fucking mean? It means you're on cloud nine. And these pyjamas are called 'Cloud Mine'. Get it now, idiot?"

We both creased with laughter.

We stopped someone and asked where there was to stay, somewhere half decent. They told us about a holiday village not too far away. We hailed a Mazda, this motortrike for carting visitors like us around and told the driver to take us there. We arrived in under five minutes. The holiday village looked like the real deal. The river on one side and a bamboo forest on the other, it had an outdoor area with a small wooden bridge, a pavilion and a barbecue pit. The rooms were yurts with everything you could ever want inside – aircon, TV, a loo. It wasn't cheap, though. Two hundred a night. But with Zhang Chao paying, it was nothing.

We booked into two yurts then went looking for a place for dinner later. There was a restaurant at the resort, but we were keen for some local homegrown fare. The same Mazda that dropped us off took us to a place nearby with a small courtyard and bamboo fencing around it. The flooring was black brick, and there was a pergola over the dining area and flowers planted about and, in front of us, the Yangtze. Not a bad place to dine. We asked the owners if we could sit out in the courtyard that evening to eat and they said they would bring out a small table. We ordered crab, shrimp, river fish, various seasonal vegetables, and cold beers, several rounds of them. We would eat first and work out the bill later. Dinner sorted, we went back to our trike driver. "Where to?" he asked. Zhang Chao said to follow the river and keep going until he said stop.

And that's what happened. We took the small roads along the riverside until Zhang Chao shouted for the driver to slow down and then, a moment later, stop. He climbed out on his own for a look around before getting back in and saying to keep going. Soon we came to a spot where there was a thicket of trees and reeds on the riverbank. Zhang Chao shouted stop. "We'll get out here," he said, paying the driver.

We stood on the high bank overlooking the river and took in what was a decent view. The small wood with its dense brush covered some ground, and the lush green slope down to the river ended at a sparse reed border that swayed in the wind. A short distance along the road stood a large willow tree and a simple hut of wood and reed thatching that looked like it must be a shop. It had rows of long benches outside the entrance and a counter displaying different drinks. Zhang Chao suggested we buy a beer, to use as a prop. We went over and picked a bench to sit on, and a young lad, who couldn't have been a teenager, stuck his head out from behind the counter and asked what we wanted. Zhang Chao bought a bottle of beer, then asked the boy for string. The boy went inside and came back out with some plastic cord which he gave to Zhang Chao. Zhang Chao fastened one end of the cord to the bottle neck and the other to a bamboo stick not quite a metre in length which he found on the ground. While he did this, Zhu Qiang and I, and the boy, all looked on curiously.

"Now I can tell you the plot. You," Zhang Chao explained, pointing at me, "sit down by the river with this bamboo pole and the bottle in the water. Act like you're having a nice relaxing time fishing. And you," he said pointing at Zhu Qiang, "you stroll along the river minding your own business, then you spot this guy fishing and walk over to have a look. The pair of you don't know each other, and you don't speak. You just fish and you just watch. Then, you'll lift the bottle out of the water and bite the lid off and start chugging. Zhu Qiang, you can't believe what you're seeing. He's not been fishing at all. He just wanted to chill the beer. When you're done," he was looking at me again now, "chuck the bottle and get up to leave, patting yourself down. Zhu Qiang, you pick up the empty bottle and turn it round in your hands to inspect it. You think you've been made fun of, so you lob the thing as hard as you can into the river. Then turn and go. That's the story. Got it?" We said we got it.

"So I'm the lead," said Zhu Qiang, sniggering. "I do the most."

I didn't see it that way, I had just as much to do as him, I thought. We started arguing about who was the star until Zhang Chao told us to shut it. "You're both the lead," he said. Not that we were really bothered about who was number one and number two, we were just pulling Zhang Chao's leg. But what did have me stumped was this story. Zhang Chao had said he had the story all laid out, and to me a story should say something, but what was Zhang Chao trying to say? I chewed this over a while but came up with nothing.

I considered asking, but didn't in the end. This might have just been a bit of fun, but I still had my self-respect, I didn't want to come off as obtuse. Also, the relationship between me and Zhang Chao had changed a little since he made his money, we were still good friends of course, but it didn't feel as easy-going as before when we could say anything. I had got used to us being close but careful at the same time. I didn't throw out the same jokes any more and I made sure to ask nothing of him, including questions. I feel like there's a lot you shouldn't ask a person after they've made it, and there are some things you really can't. Like, Zhang Chao was loaded, yes, no doubt, but how much money did he actually have – that I was curious about. I'm poor enough to be sensitive to all things money, after all. My guess put him at several million because no one with a few hundred thousand would ever be so laid back or generous. Likewise, there was no way he had anything close to tens or hundreds of millions, otherwise he wouldn't have given us lot the time of the day. Show me a single bona fide millionaire who still has any loyalty or affection. They're a cold, heartless bunch, usually. So it wasn't complete guesswork, but it wasn't the right answer either. Only Zhang Chao knew that. But how could I ask him? You can ask a pauper how much money they have, he'd be grateful for the question even, thinking you're worrying about him having enough to eat and maybe you'll help him out. But asking a rich guy, it just doesn't seem proper. What are you trying to do? Borrow some or murder him?

Zhang Chao turned on the camcorder and looked up at the branches on the willow tree, saying he wanted to record the cicadas' song. The story would have no dialogue but we should be able to hear the cicadas throughout, he said. When he was done, we left the hut and headed down the slope. "Now you know the story," he said, "this is your moment, you can show off your acting chops as best you can." But I was still wondering to myself if we knew the story at all.

Still, I found a rock to sit on and, holding up the bamboo rod, lowered the bottle into the water. It wasn't a comfortable position to hold for a long time, so I leant forward and supported myself on my knees, propping up my chin with a hand and gazing at the water. That wouldn't work, Zhang Chao said, I looked too pensive, too much like a thinker. "Relax," he said, "just pretend like you're a regular guy fishing."

I shuffled around and shifted my posture, crossing my legs on the rock and staring off at the opposite bank. I could see a low hill dotted with farmhouses. Zhang Chao didn't comment. He took off his shoes and rolled up his trouser legs, then tried a few steps into the river. The water didn't even reach up to his knees. He turned around and raised the camera. After a moment, he waved to Zhu Qiang and started to pan around in his direction. Zhu Qiang sauntered towards me and, with a few steps still to go, made like he had just noticed me there on the rock, walked over and sat down looking at the spot where my line disappeared below the water. I shot him a look like what was he doing coming over and disturbing me for no reason, but he didn't move, so I ignored him. After a couple more minutes, I fished the bottle out of the river, pulled off the cap with my teeth, wiped the bottle mouth with a hand and started to drink. With half still left, I added my own twist and offered the bottle to the wide-eyed Zhu Qiang who shook his head, no. I finished the bottle, put it down next to the rock I was sitting on, then stood up and walked away, patting down my trousers. Zhu Qiang picked up the bottle, gave it a look, then a sniff, and lobbed it as hard as he could into the river. He stood up, wiped himself off, and left.

Zhang Chao gave us his review. "Not bad, not bad," he said, "especially the part where you tried to give him the bottle. Inventive. Let's do another take." I asked him what else there was to film and he said I didn't get it. "This is what filming is like. You do several takes and pick the best one. Time for take two."

We were out of beer so I went back to the shop.

The boy stood in the entrance watching us. "Are you making a film, mister?" he asked.

I told him who we were. "I'm Jiang Wen. That's Zhang Yimou." The boy didn't react. Why would he know who Jiang Wen or Zhang Yimou was? That was a stupid thing to have said, I thought to myself.

"Mr Jiang," he said. "Why aren't you filming in town? There are lots of people there."

I told him our film didn't need many people. "Your parents?" I asked.

They had gone to work in the fields. "Mr Jiang, are there baddies in your film?" he asked. I laughed.

"No, no baddies. Everyone's a good guy."

"So it's a love story."

"Nope, not that." I didn't know how to explain. How could I when I didn't know what the film was myself?

"What are you doing? Hurry up!" This was Zhang Chao down by the river.

"I'm coming," I shouted back. I patted the boy's cheek, by way of apology for failing to give him answers, then asked him to bring me four beers in case Zhang Chao wanted to do multiple takes.

We filmed the scene again. This time both Zhu Qiang and I tried something a little different. I sat down, then stood back up shortly after and shaded my eyes with a hand to be able to see the ferry on the river. Zhu Qiang also took the beer when I offered it and handed it back after a couple of sips. Watching the video back, Zhang Chao said it was no good. "It's too busy. It should feel calm, peaceful. There can't be too much movement. Do it again, the same as the first take."

He was about to call action when two girls appeared, coming from the opposite direction on the same road we had taken. They looked like city girls, over for a day of fun. One was wearing a skirt and the other was in jeans, and they were sharing a parasol. Zhu Qiang perked up the moment he saw them. "I've said it from the start. Our film is missing women. Just think how much better it would be with a woman in," he announced, almost bellowing.

"OK. Go and get them," said Zhang Chao.

Zhu Qiang waved at the girls. "Hey, do you want to be part of a film?"

They stopped and looked at us, before leaning in to each other and conferring quietly. Then they walked on.

"You scared them off," I said to Zhu Qiang.

"A shame," he said. "We could have eaten with them after, had ourselves some fun." I told him not to worry, if they're staying in a yurt themselves we might bump into them later.

"Back to work," Zhang Chao cut in. "It's getting late."

After the third take, I lay down on the grass. "That's the last time," I said. "I'm getting wobbly."

I had downed almost three beers on an empty stomach and was starting to feel it. "Look at you," said Zhang Chao. "No dedication to the craft. And you thought being an actor was easy, eh? It's hard work."

Doing ten takes would mean ten beers, I said. "I can't drink ten beers, I'd be pissed as a fart."

"OK, let's stop," he said. "We're losing light anyway. Let's rest then go for dinner."

The pair of them plopped down next to me and opened the last two beers. We talked about the filming and Zhu Qiang straight away started blowing his own trumpet, saying how pitch perfect he thought his performance was and how he'll be shortlisted for Best Actor at the Oscars anytime now.

Bollocks, I told him, what performance? He should let Zhang Chao be the judge if he didn't believe me. "You were both passable," said Zhang Chao, "just barely. There's nothing between you. If it's good work you want to recognise, look no further than the screenwriter and director." The mention of the director started me wondering what the story meant again.

We chatted a bit longer about the film until Zhang Chao had finished half his beer and, seeming suddenly drunk, changed the topic. He told us that before coming home this time, he went to stay a couple of days in the Wannan Mountains, in a historic town called Yuliang Dam. The air was fresh, and there were good views of the surrounding mountains rising and falling into the distance. The Lian River, a tributary of the Xin'an, flowed by the town, and the ancient dam, from which the town got its name, was made of dark stone slabs, all of one colour.

Zhang Chao stayed with a fisherman's family. After dinner the first evening, he hired a fishing boat and took it upstream, to catch the views from the water. Reaching a calm stretch, he spotted a rectangular structure of bamboo poles poking through the surface and, perched on either side of it, cormorants. Their faces narrowing towards their pointed beaks, and round, beady eyes fixed on the water, each of the blackish-grey birds cut a sorry, solitary figure. "It's so late, why haven't they been taken inside yet?" Zhang Chao asked the fisherman steering the boat.

"Cormorants stink," said the fisherman. "They're not for keeping inside. They would stink out your house and the neighbours'. The smell is too much. So they're left tied on the river."

"They stay here all the time? All year round?"

"They're only let off to fish. When they're done, they're tied up again." Seeing that Zhang Chao still seemed interested, he went on, "Their meat is too fishy to eat. Someone tried it once because they didn't believe the rumours, and stank to high heaven for days afterwards. No one dared go near." Typically they live until their mid-twenties, he continued, but after twenty they're too old to catch fish any more. At that point, the kind-hearted in town will keep them and feed them on tiddlers.

"But mostly people bury them alive," he said. "Keeping them is no use if you can't eat them."

Bloody hell, Zhang Chao almost said, what a hard life. Out there on the river, rain or shine. In the dog days of summer and the harshest of winters. Standing there for twenty years only to end up buried alive.

It poured down that night and Zhang Chao couldn't sleep. Listening to rain on the roof, all he could think about were the poor cormorants still out on the river.

"Let's go," he said when he had finished telling us this. "Dinner time."

We followed the river back on foot, merry at the prospect of the feast waiting for us. I was still light-headed and walking felt more like floating, but I was enjoying myself. I looked back over my shoulder at the boy standing by the shop door watching us leave. I waved and shouted goodbye. The sun was sloping to the west and turning the sky near the horizon the colour of roses. The reflection in the water was sunset red. A small boat was bobbing and burbling on the riverbank, where it was tied up. A damp breeze blew in across the water bringing with it what I, in my tipsy state, reckoned was a rush of inspiration. It had dawned on me what our film was about. It was so very simple, and yet still so profound... It's possible that what I had in mind wasn't what Zhang Chao had intended, and was no more than my own interpretation, but right then, that wasn't what mattered.

The Dinner

Zhang Chao called me about having dinner. There would be four of us, a double date. Zhang Chao and me, obviously, and two ladies: Liu Guiru and Wang Qian. I hadn't met either of them before, but it was my job to make sure Liu didn't feel left out. I had to show her a good time, to free up Zhang Chao to put the moves on Wang Qian. This was why he called. He also wanted to lay some ground rules, like where we had to sit at the table, what we would do afterwards, who would take who home. So he wasn't calling about a bite to eat, at all.

When Zhang Chao's old lady died of cancer, the guy fell apart. He spent every day wallowing in his pit of grief in front of pictures of her hung on walls or listening to her favourite songs. He had kept her cat as well, which she had raised from being a kitten, and all of a sudden he loved that thing like he never had before. It got to the point where his dinner might be instant noodles or a couple of biscuits, but he would still make sure to go to the fishmongers in the market and bring back something tasty to boil for the cat. She was his first wife, that bond runs deep. But life goes on. Even the staunchest love fades. Everyone understands.

So eventually, Zhang Chao got back on his feet. His wife's pictures stayed up, but the heart-wrenching songs stopped filling his flat and the cat-shaped reminder of so much was relegated to the roof, ousted from its life of royal comforts to one of having to hunt sparrows and fend for itself. We had discussed the idea beforehand.

"That damn cat," he had said. "It's a nasty little thing. My wife dies and he goes mental. He's started scratching me, and he shits and pisses everywhere. The flat reeks. I can't stand it."

"What are you going to do?" I asked.

"Don't you like cats? Will you take him?"

"Na-ah, no way." I quashed that idea completely. Don't get me wrong, I like pets – the usual ones, cats and dogs – but Zhang's cat was different. It was this big, black-and-white thing, real plump with shiny fur, and as cute as they come on first appearances. But in reality it was a grump, and touchy. When I was over, the cat always squatted in the corner and eyed me gloomily, and if I made the slightest move to call or stroke him, he bolted straight under the bed or skidded across the countertops. The cat did not want me touching him. There was this one time I got so annoyed I made Zhang Chao try to help me catch him. All I wanted was one stroke. We opened a drawer and Zhang Chao held down the cat inside while I stuck out my hand to pat his head. I almost jumped out of my skin when the thing started yowling like a ghost. This was what Zhang Chao was offering for me to look after. His wife had coddled that cat like it was a baby, and treated it like her son when it got big. When she was near the end, she never forgot to remind Zhang Chao to promise he would look after it. This had been her dying wish. Zhang Chao couldn't talk about the cat without misting up.

"What do you think I should do, then?"

"Get rid. Be done with it."

"I can't let the wife down like that."

"In that case, take good care of him."

"I've got it, how about this? I put him out on the roof and don't let him back in."

"Won't he starve to death?"

"Not up there, the number of sparrows we get. He'll have plenty to eat."

Dispatching the cat seemed to be the last step in Zhang Chao finally saying goodbye to the past. He pulled himself together, shook off the dust and quickly got this twinkle in his eye like he was looking for love.

He started asking everyone he knew if they had any lady friends they could introduce. Failing that, he was out searching for lady friends of his own. It was good to see him moving on.

When he accepted an invitation to guest lecture for a month this past summer at a business academy, Liu Guiru and Wang Qian were two of his students. Liu was in her thirties, warm, but not much to look at, and married to a man who worked away. This was what I learnt from Zhang beforehand. She was the class monitor and had used the access this gave her to her teacher to show a particular interest in Zhang Chao. Wang, on the other hand, was twenty-four, curvy, pretty, modest, and had apparently never had a boyfriend. She and Liu were good friends, inseparable inside and outside the classroom. Zhang was never going to go for Liu, never mind that she was married. He found her appearance off-putting, and that is no basis for a relationship. Wang was a different kettle of fish. She was his type, exactly. Plus, as far as Zhang Chao could tell, she wasn't completely uninterested in him. He was confident that if the right opportunity came along, the pair had great potential. But he knew that getting close to Wang meant going through Liu. The alternative wouldn't be smart.

* * *

Dinner was at the Danube Restaurant. We sat in a window booth, partitioned off from others, with a view of the street outside. The lighting was soft, there was a candle lit on the table. We ordered breaded pork cutlets, pot roast, prawns and grilled fish, country-style soup, plates of vegetables, fruits and salad, a pizza and a bottle of French red.

It had all the makings of a pleasant evening, but things got off to an awkward start when Zhang Chao went in too hot. He put the whole of his attention on the pretty Wang Qian, speaking to her in hushed tones, cutting her pork for her, refilling her glass, toasting only her.

Liu and I sat there eating and sipping our drinks quietly, struggling to start up some small talk – "Do you like Western food?" "Yes, it's OK" – it was painful. The best I could manage was to touch glasses with her whenever Zhang Chao made to cheers Wang. Meanwhile, between mouthfuls, Liu stared out of the window with this forlorn look about her. I could understand Zhang's eagerness, he had been out of the game for a while and was keen to find himself a woman, and he could have done much worse than Wang. Her fringe curled down over her forehead, and she had fair skin and large eyes – oh and, that's right, decent jugs to boot. But he should have taken it easy, Liu and I had only just met, we knew nothing about each other. At the very least he should have got everyone settled in before trying to turn on the charm.

But the guy still had the cheek to shoot me a look while he was topping up Wang's glass. It was obvious what he meant by it, so I tried loosening up a little, but that was easier said than done when I was sat across from a complete stranger. If only Zhang and I had swapped places for five minutes, things would have been *very* different. Liu was all angles. She had a trowel for a face, a pointy nose and chin, eyebrows that sloped away from each other. If she'd had no make-up on, I probably would have thought nothing of it, but I could tell she was wearing foundation, and her lips were this violent red. It was weird, honestly. But I knew I ought to put on a performance or else Zhang would never let it slide. There's no talking sense with him sometimes. A man on heat doesn't have use of his head, everyone knows that. So it was lucky there was wine. To perk myself up I necked half my glass in one, refilled it and then chased a healthy piece of beef with another sip. I savoured the flavour and the moment. The wine wasn't bad. Light and supple, a little sweet, sharp, then for the finish this refreshing, delicate herby bouquet. It didn't take much imagination to feel like I'd been transported to a shaded vineyard, where chirping birdies flitted here and there, and lush French countryside stretched in every direction.

Drinking so quickly made me tipsy, but boy, did it feel good. Plus, in the candlelight, Liu came to life some more. Her pointed chin, in profile, looked almost handsome. And yes, her nose was never going to look good from any angle, but her eyes, if you really took them in, they had a sort of glint to them. If only she didn't have that sad dog look and a spindly frame. They made me feel sorry for her.

She'd done nothing wrong, though, when you think about it. She wasn't nice to look at, but was that her fault? And she liked Zhang Chao, nothing to criticise there. And just because a woman has to be beautiful to get any attention, does that really mean the less fortunate should be hung out to dry?

"You seem a little down," I said to her.

"I'm fine," she said. "This is just how I look."

"You've barely touched your wine. Come on, have a drink, it'll cheer you up."

I raised my glass and touched it against hers, and we both took a large gulp. She had no qualms with having a drink, as long as I toasted her. I topped her up again, and the two of us chatted while I occasionally toasted her. Soon her cheeks were flushing red and she was talking more. I was even starting to enjoy myself. The atmosphere around the table was better, Zhang and Wang were getting along, Liu and I were conversing. This was all happening at just the right volume. We had a proper double date on our hands, just like Zhang Chao wanted. He was all smiles now, too, leaning in close to Wang's ear, making her giggle and blush with flirty comments, which only made her even prettier. It looked like everything was going smoothly. Then his wife floated into my mind, and I wondered whether if she were a spirit up in Heaven looking down would she approve? They had been such an affectionate and loving couple, she couldn't ever have expected that before her tea had even cooled Zhang would be off in search of a new flame. There is no end to the different ways men and women can be together, the match made in Heaven is a myth.

When we had reached the bottom of the wine bottle, I asked the waiter to bring another two. They would be expensive, I knew that for a fact, but the bill wasn't for me to worry about. Liu was.

I asked about her hobbies and she said she liked to read. Contemporary literature from abroad, mostly. So we started to talk about books and shared our opinions on a few of the more obvious ones. I'd heard everything she had to say before, it was trite stuff, but I wasn't going to tell her that. I just agreed with any word that came out of her mouth. She did not extend me the same courtesy. She rejected my opinions like it was a sport. But it didn't bother me, I wasn't there for a debate, I had to keep her happy.

Zhang took her visit to the toilet as a chance to tease me a little. "You and Class Monitor Liu seem to be getting along! How about it, she's nice, right? Clever, sweet." I smiled at him. How could I respond without spoiling his chances with Wang Qian?

"Guiru is such a good person," said Wang, turning to me. "Get to know her and you'll see."

A girl with all the looks and none of the brains. Couldn't she tell I didn't care if "Guiru" was an angel or the devil?

We changed topic when Liu came back from the bathroom. I told her I had learnt to read palms from a book and offered to do hers. She said no, women have some secrets they don't want everybody to know. She even said no when I explained that it was just for fun and she shouldn't take it so seriously. I tried, anyway. So I mentioned something I thought was guaranteed entertainment: "Zhang here has a cat, but he doesn't have time to feed it or look after it. So he put it out on the roof where it can hunt sparrows, and he won't let it back in."

I went on to explain that Zhang lived on the top floor of a six-storey apartment block, which meant the cat was stuck up there with nothing but water tanks and cement slabs for company. The cat had whined all day long at first, probably from baking in the sun or being soaked by rain, not to mention it had zero hunting experience and couldn't catch a sparrow to save its life, which was the whole idea. It must have been starving. Then, one day, the mewling stopped. Zhang put this down to the cat having learnt through hardship how to fend for itself: "I mean, it's a cat isn't it, it's supposed to be free – out in the open – it's his instinct to hunt mice and birds for dinner. It's immoral to lock cats inside and feed them from a bowl." At least, this had been his argument until he went up to the roof one day so he could see how the hardened, rewilded cat was faring, and found it long dead.

This was as much of the story as I told Liu, missing out what happened next, for Zhang Chao's sake. He had wrapped the dead cat in newspaper, dropped it in a binbag, then called for me to meet him. The two of us took a taxi to Baima Hill Public Cemetery where he dug a small hole next to his deceased wife's grave and lowered the cat's corpse into it. In the taxi back to his flat, he sat, red-eyed, in silence the whole way.

Liu listened to me tell the part up to the discovery of the dead cat, then turned to Zhang Chao. "Is that true?"

Zhang had been so focused on wooing Wang Qian that he hadn't heard a word I had said. "What's that?" he asked.

"You abandoned your cat on the roof and it starved to death."

He chuckled. "That cat had been spoiled all its life,

it was useless. There are always loads of sparrows on that roof, couldn't it catch a single one?"

"What a shame. If I had known, I could have taken him."

"Is that right? Well, next time, then." But Zhang was already turning back to resume his conversation with Wang Qian.

Liu looked gutted. It was painful to see. There are all kinds of tragedy in this world. One of them is liking someone who doesn't like you back.

I was in love with a woman at work once, but her heart was already taken. I pined after her in secret, hopelessly, for two years. If I managed to talk with her or our eyes happened to meet, I would almost shake with excitement. It's still difficult to look back on that time. Just thinking about it makes me sad. So there was nothing I wanted more right then than to share my pain with Liu, but I knew that it wasn't the place.

"I've got a story I can tell you about a dog," I said, instead, trying to feel her out.

She nodded, and her expression relaxed.

I told her that we used to have a Pekinese at home, which we trained not to accept food from other people by giving it a taste of what would happen if it did. A friend of my wife's was over, and we gave her some duck liver to feed the dog. The moment it saw its favourite meal, the dog trotted up to her and swallowed the liver down in one, only we had stuffed this biggest of treats with chilli paste, so the dog spat it back up just as quickly as it went down. The dog instantly started whining and retreated under the bed with its tail between its legs. It never took food from anyone but us after that. Even ages later when I was out for a walk with it once, the dog suddenly started barking like mad and tugging at the lead like it was trying to rush someone. I looked up and there was that same friend who had fed it the doctored liver, waiting at the bus stop. She had become our dog's sworn enemy.

Liu let slip a smile.

* * *

We were nearing the end of dinner by then, but Liu stood up and said she felt dizzy from drinking too much. She was going home. Zhang's response was gruff: "What are you doing in such a hurry? Sit down, we're leaving soon, we can find somewhere for us all to go afterwards."

I also tried to encourage her to stay, but she insisted. Her head hurt. She told us to have fun.

"All right, then, you go," said Zhang Chao.

"I'll go with you," said Wang Qian, standing up.

Zhang Chao caught her by the arm. "Stay, c'mon, sit sit sit."

Wang Qian looked at Liu. She was hesitating.

"You stay and enjoy yourself," said Liu. "You don't have anything on tomorrow, anyway." Wang Qian sat down again.

I walked Liu out, seeing her to the curb outside. We were about to say goodbye when I had this sudden sense that if I let her leave just like that, it would be unfair on her. Where that idea came from I've no idea, maybe it was the drink, or it might have been the neon lights over the restaurant entrance, and the couples, all dolled up, that were filing in and out while Liu was about to walk home alone in the dark. The contrast must have moved me in some way. Mostly, I wanted her to leave with something about the night that she could take away, a feeling she would be happy to return to. But what feeling was that? I wanted her to feel what Wang Qian had. What it's like to have a man like you, to have a man pursue you. I thought for a woman that must be a beautiful feeling.

"Liu Guiru," I said, "it's been a pleasure. When are you next free? I'd like to take you out for dinner, just me and you. How does that sound?"

She said nothing for a moment as she gave me an odd look. Then she said, "Is there any need?"

Jiang Chunxiao

One morning last year, I got a phone call from a former colleague inviting me out for dinner. There would be a group of us, she said, all women except me, to welcome back another colleague who was visiting. This was Jiang Chunxiao who moved to Singapore years ago, even before I left the company. She was getting in that afternoon. I said I'd be there, it had been too long and I was pleased we'd be able to catch up and talk about old times. Though I was also surprised that they even thought of me, I admitted. She hadn't, said the colleague on the phone with a chuckle, it was Jiang Chunxiao who mentioned me and asked if anyone would be able to get in touch. She had said I should be there. This had apparently started a difficult search for my contact details, which persisted until the colleague asked a mutual acquaintance for help and they'd been able to sort them out.

Huh, so Jiang Chunxiao still thought of me – that was my first response after I put down the phone. It moved me more than I would have guessed, partly because it was so unexpected. Our relationship had been friendly but professional. What memories of it did she still cherish?

* * *

The company in question was a foreign cosmetics producer, a sizeable one, with branches in several big cities and a head office in Singapore. I was responsible for the company newsletter which went out every month or two. It contained company news like the year-end annual report, a recent visit by the Singaporean GM, new rules and regulations, introductions to newly established departments and important appointments and departures, plus product releases and ads. The remaining space was reserved for employee self-evaluations, which were never more than declarations of praise for the company by the staff and of how far hard work will get you, that kind of thing. Everyone in a management position, which meant the deputy chairman, the deputy general manager, the department and assistant managers, the factory managers and assistant managers, they were all either Chinese Singaporean, Chinese Indonesian, Chinese American, Taiwanese or Hong Kongese. Essentially, none of them were from the Mainland. There was also a stipulation for how to address them; rather than by title or role, we referred to the men as Mister and the women as Ms. So any Mr This or Ms That was a manager of some sort, and not from China. They had a dedicated break room as well as their own canteen in the food hall, were not required to clock in or out, didn't need a pass to leave the premises during work hours and weren't obliged to join morning meetings, which were mostly just for singing uplifting songs and chanting the company's own motivational slogans. They had their special stratum in the company.

My workload was light. It took me two or three days at most to complete an issue. I gave all the fiddlier tasks, like proofreading and layout, to the external prepress company. I didn't have to pay, so why not? I also made sure to drag out an issue longer than the few days necessary so as not to draw attention, everyone else hunched over their desks morning till night while I had my feet up. I would make out like I was just as busy as everyone else, staying at my desk furiously scribbling and sketching away to give the impression I had more work than I could ever finish, and no one else but me really understood how to put a newsletter together or how little effort it actually took so there were no questions.

But that was all I did, and the salary wasn't bad; it was more than double what I had earned at an actual newspaper. The only letdown was the company had strict rules, and I struggled to adjust. For one, the men were forced to wear the same standard issue suit and tie; then it was light make-up for the women, clean shaven for the men; no long hair, no shaved heads; no smoking during work hours, no snacking, no leaving your desk; no making or accepting calls unrelated to work, no doing anything that wasn't to do with work, no talking about income, no playing cards during breaks, no wearing shoes that showed any ankle in summer, no talking loudly or being noisy; managers were to always be greeted as Mr or Ms Whatever, and a manager had to sign a pass if you needed to leave for any reason during work hours because there was no sneaking out or getting past the security hires on the main gate since they had no friends and made no exceptions. There were more rules I can no longer remember, and if some of the ones above seem reasonable, then there were others I never understood. Like the alley that ran behind the company building, which was the most direct route to both the dormitory area and the food hall, being reserved for misters and missuses, while everyone else had to take the main road in front, or in other words, the long way round. In summer, the trees along that back alley provided shade, but there wasn't a single tree on the main road and the sun was merciless. It wasn't like anyone really afraid of getting burned could have taken the back way occasionally, either; the security guards on the main gate could see the alley and would shout them down: "Hey, you're not allowed down there, have you heard?"

With all that, I barely spent any time at my desk. I used to leave out dictionaries and various documents, new product instructions and balled-up drafts, alongside publicity pictures, templates and a few recent issues, so I'd look swamped with multiple priorities, and then I'd take a stroll around the office. This was a special privilege I had secured for myself. I told my manager, Ms Deng from administration, that my work required me to commission content from other staff and also teach contributors how to compose their articles, and I had to dig up worthwhile news as well so there was actually something for people to write about, and as a result I couldn't just stay chained to my desk, I needed freedom of movement. It was a reasonable ask, and Ms Deng signed it off on the spot.

Ms Deng was a plain woman in her thirties, freckled and spindly, who walked with the energy of a man. She was pretty good to me. As long as my request wasn't unreasonable, she would give it the green light. So when I requested a top-of-the-range camera, in the name of work, even though I planned to take it everywhere, or when the office was becoming stuffy and I had asked to go out for a walk, she happily said yes. Someone even grassed on me once, told her I was sneaking off for a smoke during work hours, since why else would I smell of cigarettes all of the time, and Ms Deng heard this, blinked at the informant, then told me to be careful. That was it. If that had been anyone else, their bonus that month would have been docked, at the very least. She was famously stern with people, everyone in administration feared her, but she didn't really know the ins and outs of my job, and this gave it either prestige or mystique. Her being Chinese Indonesian, part of me wondered whether newspaper editors over there were looked upon as extraordinary in some way. Another reason she acted differently with me might well have come from when the big boss visited and praised a recent issue of the newsletter he happened to read. This was the ultimate recognition of my work and was, in turn, a credit to her and her management skills. She saw me in a new light after that.

I used my privilege to flit between offices looking for people to chat with, or else to wander the factory area where I'd watch the workers in action and snap a photo here or there, to make it look like I was on the job. But my favourite location was the office building rooftop where I'd smoke and take in the views. Pujiang Economic Development Zone was still in its early days then, and in the stretches of open land not yet claimed by foreign enterprises there still grew weeds and wildflowers. Willows lined the banks of the stream to the south, and something like a transmitter station was visible on the top of a nearby mountain. I'd gaze at all this while lamenting how I'd wasted a potentially excellent youth in a worthless place and used up so much time on such a supremely boring job. I would remember, before heading back inside, to pick up all the discarded cigarette butts to drop into the drain and kick away the ash.

I eventually stumbled upon a large room in the factory area that was never locked and was filled with two-metre-by-fifty-centimetre cardboard boxes. When I came to realise there was never anyone in there, I had the bright idea to build myself a secret shelter, far back in the room, where I could sit and lie down. I could then play cards with friends until as late as I wanted and when my shift started in the morning, simply take to my little hideout to catch up on sleep.

Work became much easier to bear after that. Sometimes I would wake up and half the day was already gone. I even used it for my smoking spot since I was less likely to be spotted there than on the roof.

Another thing that's worth mentioning is the number of women in the company compared with men – loads more, essentially, and particularly young women.

That might sound like the perfect environment for a single guy like me to work my charm, but it just wasn't the place. All the girls there, pretty or not, they only had eyes for the misters. And it was understandable. The misters were the ones with the money, earning salaries umpteen times larger than mine. If they could bag themselves one, then they were headed for great heights. Two lucky ladies bore this out. One managed to woo a manager from Hong Kong who at the time had a wife but soon divorced her so he could be with our girl. The new couple then moved to Hong Kong.

The other was a young missus who found herself a manager at another company in the city, a Chinese American guy who became her ticket straight to Heaven – they had no sooner married than they were packing for the US, leaving the rest of us green-eyed. There was no mistaking it, homegrown talent like myself did not feature in the dreams of the company's most ambitious women. Though there was the odd girl with her sights set lower who would let on that she might be interested, their looks simply weren't for me.

I rarely dealt with the company's misters, our work never threw us together. At most, I'd shout a hello to Mr Whatever in the corridor, and Mr Whatever might give me a nod back, or he'd stride past with chin up and chest out, but I saw them act much friendlier with the women. Mostly, though, I didn't think of much of them. Take away their money and they were plain philistines, as far as I was concerned. Maybe that's me being narrow-minded, but I had grounds. A Mr Wong sent someone to fetch me once, shortly after a new issue came out. I couldn't imagine why. The man had been deputy GM before, the division's top boss – like I said, the GM and chairman were based in Singapore and had a different role in the corporation. At some point the GM had performed an inspection, though, and for some reason gave Mr Wong a dressing down and a kick upstairs, relegating him to the deputy chairman position where he was responsible only for the logistics department of which every branch had its own manager, and they mostly got their orders from the deputy GM. It was as good as an honorary station. Singapore also sent over a Ms Wu to serve as the new deputy GM.

Standing in front of Mr Wong's broad black desk as if to attention, I asked why he'd called me in. He tossed the most recent edition of the newsletter onto the table and said severely, "What do you call this? A character is wrong on the front page."

That surprised me. I bent down to look and asked, carefully, "Where?"

He spun the newsletter around and pointed at a line. "Look here. Here. *Ding* is *ding*, correct, but the *liu* is wrong, it's a different *liu*, it's missing the wood element."

"Oh." I inhaled sharply. "That character isn't *liu*, it's–"

"And here too," he said before I could finish, turning to the next page. "The heading of this article is too long." Now this was plain rubbish, but I nodded and didn't reply.

I left his office convinced the guy had been sitting on his arse for too long. He wanted a taste of his former power and so found me. It gave me something to laugh about for a few days, since I started concluding all my conversations by saying, "I'm very serious, my *ding* is *ding* and my *liu* is *liu*." Or: "Don't mention it. Your *ding* is *ding* and your *liu* is *liu*." No one knew what I was going on about, so the stock answer was, "What do you mean? Can I borrow the camera or not?"

"So uncultured," I said, tutting. "Can't even read."

My work often put me in contact with Ms Wu, the deputy GM, with some instructions coming straight from her, a privilege very few enjoyed. Like what to put on the front page, should I include whole or partial company documents, how big to make the pictures from the big boss's visits, should photos of other managers be included? When an issue was complete, I would send it to Ms Wu to sign off. She only ever looked at the headings and contents and made the occasional suggestion, she never said anything about wrong words. With her approval, it then went off to the prepress company. All of this was communicated via her secretary, Jiang Chunxiao. Sometimes Jiang came to find me at my desk and other times I'd go to Ms Wu's office to find her. Ms Wu's office was a large suite, where she could work behind a closed door while Jiang sat at a desk outside.

Jiang Chunxiao was in her mid-twenties and unbelievably attractive – best-looking woman in the company.

She had a round face, large eyes, a small, straight nose, fair, smooth skin, and a curvy figure. She didn't speak a great deal and walked around wearing a serious expression that looked like an attempt at dissuading any unserious suitors. Other than work, she didn't talk with me about much of anything else. It was patent that a beauty like her would be saving herself for her future mister, she was going to waste no time jabbering away with a nobody like me.

Word was that she had interest from two unmarried misters, too, but that she never made her intentions known on either front. And rightly so, a girl as pretty as her, and so well liked by the top boss, Ms Wu – Ms Wu took her everywhere, in and out of work – not just any old mister would do. She could afford to be picky.

I always tried to act as casual as possible with Jiang. I knew nothing was ever going to happen between us so what else could I do? I didn't mind that she wasn't very chatty, because once our work talk was done, I would fill the silence with whatever was on my mind. To talk away with a beautiful woman is a thing of beauty in and of itself. And she was stuck with me. I might have been an undesirable but she still had to show me basic respect and at least reply occasionally. She was from Anqing, in Anhui, and had taken the sciences track at university. She was a homebody who spent most of her time in her dormitory listening to music. She didn't exactly love her job, but she would try her best since she had it. Her plans for the future? She hadn't thought that far ahead, she had work to do first. What sort of man was she looking for? That was none of my business.

A little lost for something to say on one occasion, I pointed at the plain yellowish-white thing that was always hanging from her red bead necklace. What's that? I asked. It was an old ivory snuff bottle, she explained, the necklace was agate. I asked if she would take it off so I could have a look, and she unclipped it at the back and handed it over. It was clear the thing was old. The snuff bottle, with its rounded corners and edges, was beautifully made. Bas-relief flora and fauna adorned both faces. I removed the round stopper and found that attached to its bottom was a slender metal arm, black, that ended in a small spoon. For scooping the snuff, she said. It was nice but it wasn't especially interesting so I gave it back. She took it in her palm and gently squeezed and stroked it for a brief moment, before delicately returning the stopper and twisting it until tight. Then back around her neck went the necklace. She cherished the thing, that was apparent.

So it happened that at the end of our next work chat, when I was struggling to think up some small talk, I got a sudden urge to tease her a little. "Will you give that to me?" I said pointing at the small bottle.

She flinched as if in disbelief I'd ask such a thing, so much so she didn't know how to respond. Then she jumped up in a huff and stormed out.

Now that was an interesting reaction, and it only made me all the more eager to have myself some fun. So the next time we spoke, I tried the same line. "Will you give me the snuff bottle?"

And again, every time after. "How about it? Can I have the snuff bottle?"

Sometimes we might bump into each other in the food hall or the corridor. "When are you giving me the snuff bottle?"

At first, she would respond either by rolling her eyes at me or turning away. But later she acted like she hadn't heard. And eventually, I stopped feeling any which way about it myself, but I kept pestering her regardless, it had become like a catchphrase.

Then one morning, I had barely sat down when Jiang Chunxiao appeared in front of me and placed on my desk a bulging brown envelope. "What's this?" I asked.

"Take a look."

I picked the envelope up and, unfolding the flap, stuck my hand inside.

I pulled out the red agate necklace with an ivory snuff pot attached. I looked at her chest where hers had always hung and it was bare.

"For you," she said.

"What? What happened?" I was confused. For a moment, I didn't know what she was up to.

"I'm leaving," she said, "so I want to give you this."

"You're leaving, where to?"

Without answering, she turned and walked away.

But I soon found out where she was going and why. She was Singapore-bound, to marry Ms Wu's cousin. This was normal, though, wasn't it, I didn't feel like I had lost out. In this business, a pretty woman like her belonged to the misters.

I left the company myself only six months later. I had been discovered sleeping on the job.

After a long night of cards, I retreated to my cardboard hideout for a nap. I slept so soundly I started to snore. Two workers collecting boxes heard and followed the sound to its source, then reported me. When I was woken up, I drowsily climbed out of my secret lair and the first thing I saw was Mr Ma from the factory. I had really done it now. Not even my usual champion Ms Deng could save me. I was let go with immediate effect.

* * *

The evening of the meal last year, I got stuck in traffic and arrived at the restaurant much later than arranged. My old colleagues had already started eating, in the private room. Almost twenty years had passed and all the girls and young women of back then were now middle-aged. One of them was even visibly greying, and it wouldn't have been an exaggeration to call her an old woman. Jiang Chunxiao's appearance surprised me most of all. I was expecting to see a heavily bejewelled kept woman. But instead she wore a buttoned batik jacket of white flowers on blue, no make-up and no earrings or jewellery of any sort. She was on the slim side, pale, and her forehead was starting to show wrinkles. There were bags under her once twinkling eyes, and she looked altogether worn out. A faded beauty. She might have been any average woman of that age you would see in the street – though she still had a certain poise, I just couldn't connect her with the image in my head of the spoiled Chinese Singaporean wives of the wealthy.

She gave me a warm welcome and directed me to the empty chair next to her, asking the waiter to bring a beer which she poured for me herself. The women were drinking coconut water.

I raised my glass and toasted each of them in turn, and then rued how quickly time had passed, saying how everyone was unrecognisable from all those years ago and how I wouldn't know them had we passed each other in the street. Then another toast, to our lost youth.

They asked how things were going, and I asked them the same. Those who lived in the city but had lost touch had all at some point left the cosmetics company; in the financial crisis that had swept across the globe in recent years, the company had had to withdraw to Singapore to reduce costs. Two of the group were already retired, and one other had been laid off when her company started struggling. A fourth had started her own housekeeping business, which was only small but doing well.

Jiang's situation was unexpected. She had divorced some years before and had been back in China ever since. No wonder she didn't look the part of the kept wife, she wasn't one. But that wasn't all: she didn't have kids and hadn't remarried, and she hadn't found another job when she came back.

"How do you make a living?" I asked.

"I barely spend anything. I only buy food, and I don't eat much. My boyfriend lives with me and he earns enough to cover the rent for our small place.

That's plenty for me." She said all of this so calmly. I struggled to believe what I'd just heard: she lived with her boyfriend. She had said that, out loud. I looked her over and tried to pick out in her current appearance the Jiang Chunxiao I had once known.

"So you at stay at home all day doing nothing?" I asked after a moment.

"No, I paint."

"Paint? Since when did you paint?"

"My uncle is a painter, I've always liked painting because of him. My parents didn't approve, they thought it would interrupt my studies, so I stopped. When I came back from Singapore, I picked it up again."

"Do you sell them?"

"No, it's just for enjoyment."

"Do you know any other painters?"

"Not really, I'm not very social. I prefer to stay at home and work on pieces, or go to exhibitions. That's why I'm here, there's a Ming and Qing art exhibition on in the city."

The women were more concerned about her not having children. Not marrying wasn't an issue, they said, and nor was living with a boyfriend – these women were open-minded! – but they struggled to understand the not wanting a child. They all clamoured to ask why she hadn't had one when she was younger. Her life would be different with a child, they said, she would have someone to look after her in her old age, but most of all she would have someone to whom she could pass on her life. One of them even suggested it might not be too late.

Jiang stayed silent for a moment. "You might find it hard to believe," she said eventually, "but there are some things I just understood too late. Like, where a kid comes from. How old were you when you found out? For me it was university. And when I knew, I thought it was so dirty, so disgusting, I couldn't bear the thought. I vowed then that I would never give birth."

Of course, this wasn't the reason the women had expected and they all went quiet. No one seemed to know what to say. They glanced between each other as though thinking, Aren't we also women, why didn't we ever have that same thought? To be honest, it was new to me too.

I had heard all sorts of justifications for not having a kid. The typical ones I won't say here, but there have been weird ones too. One friend said that the world is too chaotic, it didn't feel a safe place in which to raise a child. Another explained, "Do you know your grandad's name? If so that's not bad, but do you know his dad's name, or his grandad's name? Of course you don't, you're as good as strangers, and the same goes the opposite way, you never think of them and you certainly don't love them. You've no connection with them at all. So why should I kill myself contributing to a line of people with no connection to me? Do I have nothing better to do? It's not for me. I'm stopping it before it starts." I ought to say that these two friends, though their reasons are eccentric, I can still understand their points of view, but Jiang Chunxiao's?

"And your boyfriend agrees?" This was the grey-haired colleague.

"Yes, he agrees." This was an unhelpful response. She gave me the impression she didn't want to continue with the topic.

"Jiang Chunxiao," I said, starting on another, "do you still remember that snuff bottle you gave me?"

"Of course," she said, "how could I forget? I adored that thing. It was my grandmother's."

"It was an antique?"

"Yes, do you still have it?"

"I've kept it all this time," I said. In reality, I lost track of it ages ago. I moved house multiple times and I either gave away or chucked out everything I had no more use for, the snuff bottle included. Maybe I had given it to someone, I didn't remember. But I wasn't going to tell her that.

"I still get it out sometimes to admire," I added, "and when I do I think of you." This part was obviously a joke.

"Well, I should think so," she said, laughing. She knew it was a joke. She patted me lightly on the arm as she took a sip of coconut juice. "That bottle used to be my grandmother's. She came from a wealthy family of some influence. Her great-grandfather on her dad's side was an imperial scholar in the Qing dynasty, a magistrate. I still remember when I would go to her place in the countryside as a child. She had this big house with two stone lions guarding the door like they do. It had swooping eaves, stepped gables. Oh, and this ancient tree peony in the courtyard which was planted in a blue brick flower bed. It was taller than most people. Grandma used to say the plant came into the family with one of her grandmothers, during the Qianlong reign, yet it still blossomed even after all this time. In spring when it flowered, people used to travel from far and wide to see it. The peony was famous in the area. I've seen it myself, the shrub all in bloom. It was gorgeous."

She became more excited as she spoke and her gradually flushing cheeks gave her face an alluring glow.

I raised my glass. "Come on," I said, "to your grandmother, and also to that Qianlong-era tree peony. Cheers."

* * *

This last spring, some friends and I took a road trip out to Wannan. Before we set off, I had the idea to give Jiang

Chunxiao a call. I had taken down everyone's numbers at the dinner.

I told her our plan and itinerary, and said that if time allowed, we would maybe take a detour to Anqing for a couple of days, mostly so we could see her family's hometown and see that tree peony for ourselves. Would she be able to join us? I asked. Yes, she said, if we made it there she would definitely come along, it had been ages since she had seen her hometown or the shrub. Now felt like the time, and it was the right season.

She sounded pleased. I had been apprehensive to start with, in case she said no, we weren't close friends after all, but I hadn't expected she would agree so quickly. I couldn't say why but I found myself fascinated by the idea of the place. Just picture it, this age-old home where generations upon generations of family had lived, and in their mossy courtyard there is a tree peony from the High Qing era in full flower, isn't that sort of magical? I even imagined that come nightfall, my friends and I, and Jiang Chunxiao, might all sit around a table in the courtyard next to the resplendent shrub.

The moon high and bright, the dim silhouettes of flowers in the courtyard, a subtle perfume wafting around us, we'd drink and talk about times long past. What a lovely evening it would be.

It was a shame, then, that we didn't make it in the end. The others I went with to Wannan were opposed.

What was so good about a tree, they said, it doesn't matter which dynasty it's from, there are old trees everywhere. I had nothing to say in reply. I texted Jiang Chunxiao the reason we weren't going and she seemed disappointed. If I ever had time in the future, she said, I should go on my own and she would join me, take me to see her hometown and the peony.

She even called me a while later. It was one evening when I was playing cards in a bar. Her voice was quiet and I had to strain to hear. She sounded unsure about having called.

I asked if anything was wrong, but she reassured me there wasn't, she was just looking for someone to talk to.

"Why's it so noisy there?" she asked. I told her. "Ah," she said, "let's talk later, then, I'll call you." But she never did.

And slowly, I forgot her.

Then one morning in mid-autumn, I was recovering from a hangover, my head still heavy and not feeling my best. I took my phone from the bedside table and opened it to find a text message. It was from the same colleague who had invited me to the dinner last year. There was just one line: Jiang Chunxiao died yesterday, suddenly.

Guinea Pigs

It was late and raining. Nobody was going to call and drag me out now. I opened a bottle of wine to enjoy to myself.

I finished the bottle and went to lie in bed, content, listening to the pitter-patter of the rain outside and letting random snatches of welcome memory carry me off. Then the phone rang. A call from Old Fang saying he was in a bar, and would I join him? Normally, after a drink, I never much feel like leaving the house, especially not on nights as dreary as that one had turned out, but Old Fang is an old friend. I said no a few times, then replied I wouldn't be long.

At the bar, Old Fang was sat at a table with a man and a woman. The man, a young guy with high cheekbones and big ears, looked like the type who wrote poetry. We'd met before, and it ruined my mood seeing him there. The woman was twenty-six maybe, a dainty little thing and pretty with it. Straight away I liked how she carried herself.

"You made it," Old Fang called over. Meng Long, the young guy, said hello like he was desperate for me to like him. Then he introduced the girl, Huang Qian. She must have been with him. Why she was mixing with a boring loser like him was a mystery to me.

I sat down and ordered a chrysanthemum tea, taking off my jacket. The heating in the bar was on high. "How've you been?" asked Old Fang.

"Same old, same old," I said, reaching for the packet of cigarettes on the table and taking one.

"But like I said, I just can't get enough." This was Meng Long, who looked at Old Fang and then at Huang Qian. He was picking up where he had left off. "I waste no time when I'm with a woman. We're straight into bed together." He gave Huang Qian what he probably thought was a cheeky wink.

Fucking hell, this guy is the worst, I thought. I turned away and looked out the window. It was still raining, only drizzling now, though. The waterlogged road had a petrol-slick sheen. Two people with brollies hurried past. In the corner shop across the road, the middle-aged assistant was staring into thin air, with her elbows on the counter and her chin in her palms.

Meng Long was still talking. "...I'm telling you, any girl who comes over, she sees all the naked women on the wall, and all she wants to–"

"It's boiling in this bar, isn't it?" I cut in, turning back to the three of them.

"I'm all right," said Old Fang. "Sounds like you've already had a drink?"

"You got me there. A bottle of red at home."

Old Fang smiled, shaking his head. "I've never understood why you always drink on your lonesome."

"I don't like getting too close with people. And you know yourself that whenever there's a get-together and drinking's involved, sooner or later someone will start mouthing off and talking big. It makes me uncomfortable."

"You're not a big lover of the human race, are you?" Old Fang was only half-joking.

"You're too rational." This was Huang Qian.

I glanced at her. It was the first time I'd heard her speak. I didn't agree with what she had to say, but I could tell she was a girl who got it. This only made me fonder of her, and also more confused why she was with a guy like Meng Long.

"There was this one time I had to go to Sichuan for something or other," I continued. "A bunch of friends there invited me for food, and you can bet we drank a lot, but then they all started holding hands. Some of them, when they were talking to me, they'd grab my hand and squeeze it real tight and wouldn't let go. It made my hair stand on end. Think about that, all these men holding each other's hands, all giddy and excited. What would that look like to you? A mess, right? That was what did it. I haven't drunk with anyone since."

While I talked I noticed that Huang Qian was paying close attention to what I was saying, even nodding at me when I turned to look her way as if to say she would have felt the same if she had been in my position. "Sounds like some of your Sichuan friends might be a little homosexual," said Meng Long. I didn't plan on giving him the time of day, though. I was waiting for Huang Qian to say something, but she didn't.

"It's not unusual to have those inclinations. Lots of people do," said Old Fang, between sips of his beer. "It doesn't necessarily mean they're gay." He might have only been saying this so Meng Long wasn't left hanging. He must have already picked up on my dislike for the guy and was probably regretting ever asking me to come. Maybe this was why he started to tell the story he did, to try to lighten the mood or shift my attention off Meng Long. Old Fang was a university professor, so he had a bellyful of stories about students.

This is the one he told us: There was this first-year girl, with great marks, doing well in all her modules, and really pretty too, but she kept guinea pigs. She absolutely loved them, had a dozen at least in her shared room, where she kept each one in a separate cage under her bed, all nice and in order, and fed them leafy greens every day. But the other girls in the accommodation, they eventually grew sick of sharing their space with the guinea pigs. They said they're dirty and they stink. So they asked her to get rid of them. But she ignored the girls, so they decided they had no choice but to tell staff, who found the girl and told her to deal with the guinea pigs. Animals are not allowed in university accommodation. Still, the girl doesn't listen. She kept the guinea pigs exactly as they were. So one teacher told her that if she didn't cooperate, there would have to be disciplinary action, to which the girl replied, For what? Where in the university's rules does it say that guinea pigs are not allowed in university accommodation? It would be unfair to punish her for breaking a rule that is nowhere in the school policy. And, of course, there was no rule that said verbatim that the rooms were off-limits to guinea pigs. So anyway, the teacher said while there might not be a rule about that exact thing, it was unsanitary to have guinea pigs in the rooms, and they also smelled bad. And to this the girl said that didn't make sense either, because she laid newspaper under the guinea pigs' cages and changed it regularly, so there was zero hygiene risk, and when it came to smell she would say that the smells coming off her roommates were much worse than any smell from her guinea pigs. At this point, the teacher realised that they were getting nowhere with the student and, having other duties to deal with, decided, for now, to let the matter lie. Then, for no obvious reason, one of the guinea pigs died. Not nice, no, but the girl put the dead guinea pig on a plastic sleeve on her table and proceeded to dissect it with a knife.

Now, that's a step too far for the other girls. Seeing the bloody guinea pig sliced open on the table, its insides all on show, it was too much to take. They lost it, and went straight to the top, to the president of the university. The president heard what they had to say and exploded as well, giving two instructions then and there: for the guinea pigs to be got rid of, and for the girl to write a self-criticism which she had to pin up on the school noticeboard for everyone to see, or she'd be kicked out. This time the girl did what she was told. She wrote a self-criticism in her very best Classical Chinese, and beautifully so, too, then she asked to be allowed time off so she could take the remaining guinea pigs back to her parents outside the province.

We left the bar past midnight. The air felt fresh now the rain had stopped and there were puddles on the ground. There was no one else out in the street. The woman in the corner shop opposite watched us leaving, probably hopeful we might go in and buy something. A taxi stopped a little down the street from us, and Meng

Long and Huang Qian went to take it. I couldn't work out if it was Meng Long who'd asked her back to his or vice versa. But that was when we had what I would call the evening's first and only "incident". As Meng Long opened the taxi door and climbed inside, Huang Qian, who was standing behind him, moved one hand behind her back and used it to wave at me. Old Fang was stood off to the side a few metres away looking to see if any more taxis were coming, so the wave could only have been for me. It was a funny gesture. I couldn't decide if it was meant as some sort of joke or if it had another meaning. Once they had both got into the taxi, Old Fang said, "Are you OK? You didn't seem with it tonight."

I didn't answer. Instead, I told him I enjoyed his story.

"Yeah? That really happened."

Another taxi pulled up to the curb, and I let Old Fang take it. This left me in the street alone, waiting for a ride and thinking to myself, that girl sure was odd.

Stand Firm, Stand Firm

I met this poet at a teahouse once, a friend introduced us, a skinny, pale guy, penniless he was. Something he said has stuck with me ever since. "To stand firm is everything," he said. And he was right. He was living proof. How much he had stood firm through his life sort of radiated from him. Somehow he made abstract concepts like belief, worth, ambition, endurance and survival make sense. When he said it, it was obvious he was strong of mind.

That's the sort of strength people need nowadays when the world is preoccupied with material stuff. We can't do without it. We have to stand firm. It's inspiring to think about, that level of mental fortitude, but mostly it takes me back to this experience I had.

I've been pretty consistently weak-willed in life, but

there was one occasion when I managed to stay strong. So when in that teahouse the scraggly poet I'd just met said in a voice thinned likely by hunger, "To stand firm is everything", I really, truly felt that. We had both of us, at some time in our lives, stood firm. The only real difference was that, while I had managed it just the once, he might well have been doing it every single day since he was born.

I'll add here that I've never seen the poet again since the teahouse encounter. I couldn't say how he's doing, whether he's still as radiant as ever or if he starved to death a while back.

* * *

So, back in the spring of '86, my wife at the time, Long Long, decided she wanted to see Yunnan Province. Me being her husband, I was duty-bound to help her. There was the money to get together for the trip, and I also wrote to a writer friend in the capital, Kunming, to ask if he knew anywhere she could stay. Long Long was a simple girl. Her favourite thing to do was travel, but her family's financial situation had never allowed it. When we married, what brought her the most happiness was to head out on an adventure. She would quit her job if it meant she could go. She was making up for lost time. And though I'm not made of money, and I wouldn't have said we were even doing that well back then, I had worked hard enough for long enough, and scrimped and saved wherever I could, that I did at least have something put aside. And I was all for handing over the lot in the name of love. Happy wife, happy life, let's not be coy about it. The only thing was that I could never join her. My finances only stretched so far, so I just sorted the bits I could for her from home. And anyway, I had a job to keep up if I was going to make sure there was always enough left over for Long Long's next jaunt. That was what I told myself when I had been in the office so long my head hurt: think of Long Long enjoying herself in some gorgeous place right that very moment. It was the boost my spirit needed.

So Long Long went to Kunming. There, my writer friend, a loyal mate, had arranged to put her up, and for his wife to show her the city's sights. When he heard that Long Long was planning on going to Ruili next, he even went out of his way to put her in touch with a friend of his who lived there. This friend was military, part of some regiment or other based in Ruili. He sorted it so Long Long could stay in one of the guest lodgings on site, free of charge. He also volunteered to be her guide for the few days of her stay.

Now, something happened during this part of the trip. This military man in Ruili turned out to also be from our hometown, and having someone from his old home come to visit his new home, naturally, he was extra nice to her. Too nice. At one spot he took her, navigating slippery rocks over a stream, he took her arm so she wouldn't fall. All good. But then, he didn't let go once they were across. He held on until Long Long saw he was distracted and yanked her arm free. And that wasn't all. On her last evening there, he went to her lodgings and asked her for her address, saying he'd take her out the next time he was back home. Then he started on about literature and the writing he did – he was the regiment's publicity officer and wrote fiction in his spare time – and then about how lonely it was to live on the base so far from home. He was spilling his heart. He said he would always remember the few days they'd spent together. Apparently, he just yapped on and on until Long Long started to drop hints that it was late and she wanted to get some rest. But still he wouldn't zip it. He dragged out the goodbye and said he'd be sad to see her go, and he even tried pulling a little stunt, asking Long Long for a farewell hug. She let him down gently.

When Long Long told me about this little incident, I can't say I wasn't pissed off that this so-called friend of a friend had made a move. But at the same time, I kind of got it. An attractive girl like Long Long, baby-faced and innocent as she was, a guy's got to take his chances where he can with a woman like that. He has to flirt with her at the very least. It's normal. What counted was that Long Long remained chaste for me, that was everything. I was thankful.

* * *

The summer of '88 was the next time Long Long went away. It was to the picturesque Beidaihe, where she met some handsome travel-loving Yankee and fell in love, just like that. They wasted no time getting wild together. Turns out staying chaste has a limit too. No book-loving Chinese soldier was ever going to compare to a chiselled American man. At least I could see that. So my marriage to Long Long came to an end. Naive little Long Long had wrung my savings dry, lumped me with some serious debt, then flown off with her American lover. Now she had free rein to travel around the US or the rest of the world as much as she liked, something she had been dreaming about for a very long time. So it was unexpected when a few years later a letter came from France, saying she had left the American – he might have had looks but he dragged his heels when it came to proposing – and was now married to a handsome Frenchie. But the biggest surprise was that she didn't sound as happy as I'd expected her to be. In her letter, she said the new husband was a deviant – he wasn't like this when they first met, back then he'd been gentle. He never let her go travelling. In fact, he locked her in the house and wouldn't even allow her to see the neighbours. If she didn't listen, he hit her and didn't let up. She also said she was running out of hope, she thought of death often, and if it wasn't for her daughter, she might have ended it already. And then she said that sometimes, in the quiet of night, she thought of me, about how good I was to her.

It hurt to read all of that. But also, if I'm completely honest, I almost felt smug too. Needless to say, that was much later...

My darling Long Long had left me – but life goes on. One Sunday afternoon, I was in the middle of this documentary travel show – my way of sharing in Long Long's greatest joy – when there was a knock at the door. I switched off the TV and went to see who it was. Waiting on the doorstep was a short, tanned man in a white shirt. He looked about thirty. I asked him what he wanted. He smiled and said, "You're whatsisface, Long Long's partner."

I said I was, but who was he?

Zhou Kang, he said. He had been in the military, in Ruilin. Long Long had stayed with him when she was there. It all came back to me very quickly. "I know you," I said. "Come in, take a seat."

I led the way into the living room and told him to make himself comfortable while I got him some tea. I'm not a petty man, and I'm definitely not unreasonable.

This Zhou Kang might have once tried to make a cuck out of me, but he hadn't succeeded. I hadn't lost out in the end. He had given Long Long a place to stay, and she had been my wife then. I owed him in a way, for indirectly helping me out. At the very least I could welcome him in.

Zhou Kang sipped his tea and looked around the room. "Is Long Long here?" he asked.

I answered him straight: Long Long had divorced me and moved to America. By which I meant that if he still had designs on her, he would have to move his arse to the USA. He was getting nothing out of me. I watched surprise flicker across his face and his mouth twitch like he was about to ask something but then thought better of it. After a long moment, he said he had left the army and now worked at a radio factory, but it wasn't really for him. So he had come to see Long Long and me. He remembered that Long Long had said I write, and wondered if I knew anyone in the culture sector who I didn't mind asking if their company was looking for people.

I did have friends in the culture sector, I told him, but none of them were in charge of anything, and they weren't all that useful. But I would ask and see, for him.

I was just trying to get him off my case, of course. Asking my friends to help link this relative stranger with a job that satisfied him was still well beyond the remit of our relationship, if it could even be called that.

The topic moved on to our shared friend in Kunming. We found we had a lot more in common there. We talked all the way to dinner-time, when I started asking myself whether the idea of inviting him for food was within "the remit". It would be a good way of returning a favour, I thought. So we went down to the little eatery right outside my building and had a couple of drinks with the meal while we chatted about books. His view was that literature should give people an ideal to aspire to, uphold the spirit of the times, and it should do all it can to show the real good in people. Well, OK.

* * *

It was about a week later, around eight-ish, when I was on the toilet for the third time that evening with diarrhoea after a streetside dinner of dumplings, when there was a knock at the door again. I had just been getting ready to have to sit there extra long so I wouldn't have to be up and down the rest of the night. I was about to shout for whoever was knocking to wait a moment, when I heard that person call my name. I listened again and thought, Fuck, it's that Zhou Kang again. And then, Why's he come back? Was he following up about job openings, or did he want to continue our literature chat?

At dinner, he did seem to have more he wanted to say. Whatever it was, I didn't want to see him. Our debt was settled. If he still felt he was owed something, then he only had to go to the US and find Long Long. I could only call it a day. But as I was thinking on it, I realised that actually, really, it ought to have been him who owed me. I had spared him a dressing down, after all. Yet he wouldn't let me be. Where was the sense in that?

I quickly weighed up my options and decided to ignore him. Let him knock, I thought, he'll try a few times, think no one's in, then scram. He was still calling my name, too, but he wasn't going to hear a peep out of me. I sat there on the toilet in silence, trying not to move too much, waiting for him to give in any time now. He shouted two or three times, then stopped. Then I heard a sort of scuffling sound, real quiet, which for a moment left me baffled, like what the hell was he up to, and then it clicked.

At this point, I should explain that my flat is a two-bed. The front door opens into the living room, with the two bedrooms on the right and, on the left, the kitchen. The bathroom – as in right where I bloody was – is directly across from the entrance door. So in other words the front door faces the toilet. Now usually that wouldn't be an issue, only right down the centre of the peeling front door was a blooming great crack through which a person could see into or out of the flat. I had been planning to get a new door for a while, but I was struggling to bring myself to part with the money when I came up with the idea of sticking newspaper over the inside of the crack, to cover the hole. Except, somehow, I had kept forgetting to.

My predicament was clear. That pain-in-the-arse Zhou Kang had seen light coming out through the crack and applied the most rudimentary deduction to conclude that if there was a light on inside, then someone was in – and why weren't they responding? So to double-check, he now had his face pressed to the crack and was peering inside. And what did he see?

The bathroom door open and me on the loo, with my pants around my knees. Of all the things, that was what he saw. I wanted the toilet to swallow me up. He had caught me with my pants down trying to trick him. And now he was knocking again. Of course he was knocking again, he had already seen me.

What was I supposed to do, then? Admit defeat and answer? I would have had to explain my behaviour only moments before. Tell him, "Friend, I'm sorry, I was in a bit of a bind, a particularly sensitive situation, and it was inconvenient to reply." What a pile of shit. But I couldn't think of anything more sensible. There was no way to take back my actions anyway, I just had to follow this road to its end.

He stopped knocking and started shouting again. It

was getting to me that he could be so stubborn. Why is this guy like this, I remember thinking. Wasn't it clear I didn't want to go to the door? Why be so brazen? I didn't owe him anything, we weren't even friends. I didn't want to see him, so what? What was he going to do about it? Being angry only made me more determined to sit tight right there on the toilet. I knew he was looking, so let him look, I decided. I might have been shitting in plain view but I still had my dignity.

It went on like this for a while. He would knock a few times, holler some more, then knock again, and I sat there like a sculpture carved from wood. I didn't move a muscle, didn't break wind. We couldn't have been more than five metres apart, one wooden door with a hole in it between us. He was staring at me, I was staring at the wall. Minutes went by. In my head I was repeating, Stand firm, Stand firm. It got to the point where I came over all dizzy from being so mad and from exhaustion, probably because of the diarrhoea. I had the chills, I was sweating profusely. I felt like I was going to collapse, but I gritted my teeth and stayed put. Stood firm.

And in the end, it worked. After what must have been twenty minutes, there was the sound of footsteps leaving. I strained to hear until the steps were gone.

He never came back after that.

* * *

Then not long ago, another letter arrived from France. Long Long says she's already left that piece-of-work husband. In the divorce, he got custody of their daughter. So it's just her again. She asked how I'm doing, if I'm with anyone. She said she sees now that she was unfair to me. She's sorry, and she hopes I can forgive her. At the end of the letter she said she wonders whether, were she to leave France and come back to China, I would still want her.

I was moved. I have a girlfriend now, and we'll be married soon, and there's no way whatsoever that me and Long Long would ever get back together. But I know, in my heart of hearts, that what I had with Long Long was special. Time won't change that.

The Lock

I wrote a story recently that got good reviews from all my friends. That's a rare thing for me, and it left me feeling pretty pleased, so every few days I found myself going back through the plot in my head, just to experience again that tiny jolt of success.

I wrote about my parents, my mum and my dad, about the messy relationships I've had with women, about my gifted son whose IQ is 150. The story is mostly fictional, but there's a shade of reality to it. My son is a genius, for one. But the part about my bad luck in romance is pure fantasy. To start with, I would have to have a girlfriend. I did used to, or else how would I have got my son? But she left me and I haven't found a woman who's right for me since. I've been on my own all that time while my son lives with my parents in another city.

As for the story, a friend even called me to say how much it moved him after he spotted it in a magazine. He was chatting about this and that part, then suddenly he asked, "Have you really been with so many women?"

"Not even close," I replied.

"But," and he sounded almost contemplative when he said this, "what you wrote, that must have taken some imagination."

It was not until after we said goodbye that I thought about his confusion and had to ask myself how someone like me who lives like a monk could write about relationships so believably. Why am I so committed to putting all this made-up stuff about me getting with women into my fiction? This isn't the only story I have like this. I suppose I can't discount the possibility it's my only way of scratching that itch. I could definitely reel off plenty of other pompous reasons why I write, but there's one I won't say out loud: in my writing, I can create the life I want but can't lead. It's not the wrong reason, I don't think – I wouldn't shout about it, but it is a way to let off steam and has definitely given my stories more spice. Plus, if I only wrote straight from life, how interesting could the result really be?

Imagine a story that described every little detail of someone's day, and that was the whole piece: what and when they ate, how long they slept, what they did at work, every piss and fart. Would anybody want to read it? But that's the reality of life. We might not like it, but it's the truth. Even if life manages a rousing moment every once in a while.

That reminds me of this girl, actually. I've never mentioned her to anyone before, and I haven't tried to write her into any stories either. The stuff of stories should be more exciting, more head-on than this because everything about her was just so inconsequential. But a few months back, the little shop in the entrance to my building installed a glasses counter, probably linked to some opticians in the area. It was on your lefthand side as you entered and stuck out like a sore thumb. That spot had been empty before. The wall behind the counter was covered with different pairs of specs and, next to them, this picture of a foreign lady with glasses on. The girl in question was the tiny stand's only staff member, and I didn't need glasses to see how good-looking she was. She wasn't a year over twenty, looked slim in her long green coat and had smooth, glowing skin. Under her tallish forehead, it seemed like she might have had some jaw work done. Then there were these just captivating eyes. The counter was newly opened and hardly ever had any customers. She appeared fed-up most days, slumped over the counter with a dejected look on her face, watching all the customers as they walked in and then out of the shop without making a stop by her stand. Something about her really moved me.

I was going in every day to buy a bottle of wine, out of habit. I'd start writing in the morning, or if not writing then reading, and keep going until four in the afternoon, then go out for a walk for an hour and nip in on my way back to pick up the wine, so I could get a little tipsy while I ate. Tipsy is my favourite thing to be. I can lie in bed all drowsy while I watch TV or try out some chess moves, then slowly drift off. Those had been my days for as long as I could remember, but they changed a little after I set eyes on that pretty face. My post-walk trip to the shop was no longer just about the wine. I would wander the aisles like I was looking for something and pause whenever I found somewhere unobtrusive that gave me a good angle to look at her. Soon it became obvious that she had noticed me back, probably because I was in every day. When I entered and left the shop, she always glanced at me, almost carelessly. What a treat that was to be caught in a gaze like hers. But there was no telling if she felt similar towards me, or if she just thought I was a weirdo. I couldn't imagine what I looked like in her eyes, though not for lack of trying, and I was afraid it was some pitiful sod, a drunkard who only left the flat to buy his daily dose, and a slovenly one at that, always wearing the same fading cowboy suit and a fat pair of candlewick corduroy trousers long out of fashion like I do, his skin slack on account of the drink. How different the two of us were. Just thinking about it always ruined my mood. So this became another habit of mine, taking a lap of the shop at the same time every day so I could see this pretty woman. It brought me some peace of mind. But I never went any further. I never went up to the counter or found some excuse to strike up a conversation.

I know this sort of thing can never lead to anything. She can't have been too much older than my son, what was I even thinking we'd do? I know what romance is, and I know where it ends up. So what we had wasn't bad. Seeing her was enough to leave me content.

But then I went in one day and she wasn't there. In her place, behind the counter, was some middle-aged woman with a hawk face. And the next day, and the day after. I haven't seen her since, and I don't think I ever will for as long as I live. Does she ever think of me?

* * *

This was just before my son's winter holidays. As soon as his school broke up, I put down everything and went to see him.

I have always visited in the holidays. My son started living with my parents ten years ago, when he was two.

My dad is an army veteran, a retired officer, and my mum a doctor, long retired herself. I'm their only son, though I have an older sister. They spoil their only grandson rotten, that goes without saying. When I got to theirs, I spent every minute possible with my son. We played lots of Go and computer games, and he was spared from the additional studying my parents usually assign him – with my permission, of course. They grumbled a little at first, but since I was rarely there, they kept things respectful. I was giving my son an education too. Usually this was when we went out to walk off dinner. He has a 150 IQ, I mentioned that already. He's a smart lad, which sometimes makes me wonder whether it's worth trying to teach him anything. There was this one time when we had got onto talking about cars for some reason and he said he really liked them and that he hoped he could have his own little car someday. "What makes you say that?" I asked. "It's fine to hope to have a car of your own one day, but what do you think will happen once you do? You'll start thinking about getting your own flat. Then it'll be something else, and something else. There's no end to it. It's not a good way to look at things, life isn't about the things we have."

This upset him a little. "I knew you were going to say that. I guessed every word, exactly," he said.

I hadn't expected this response, but I knew straight away that I should stop pushing my values on my son. If a kid can know right from wrong, like an adult, then that's great. But he won't be all cute and innocent any more, like a kid, will he? "You're right," I said, apologising. "Baba's saying what *he* thinks. But you're right, having your own car must be convenient. You can go play where you want when you want to. If we had a car right now, Baba would drive you to the countryside so we could have an adventure."

"I like the cars with really long bodies," he said, getting excited now. "Do you know that car's name?"

I had to leave before the holidays ended. A magazine editor had commissioned me to write a piece on beauty contests and the deadline was coming up. I had to get back and fire it off. Then the evening before I was supposed to go, something happened.

My son and I had finished dinner and gone out for our usual stroll. While we walked, I shared with him whatever thoughts came to mind, and promised that next time I would try to stay longer. We were out for about half an hour. Back at the door, my son took out his keys and started to feel about for the keyhole, since the corridor light was broken and it was dark. After some fumbling, he managed to insert the key and turn it, but then the door didn't open. "Huh? The lock's not working," he said.

I told him to knock, which he did, a few times, then

a moment later my dad was opening the door from the inside, saying, "Forgot your keys?"

"Grandad, the lock's broken. It doesn't open." While my son was saying this, I was already looking at the door in the light from the living room. Where there should have been a lock mechanism there was just a plain hole.

"The lock's gone," I said. My dad bowed his greying head to the hole to take a look.

"No wonder it doesn't open," said my son.

My mum, hearing all the fuss, popped her head out of the inner room and said "What is it?"

"The lock's been nicked," said Dad standing upright again.

Realising how serious this might be, I asked my son, "Did you notice if the lock was there when we left?"

He nodded. "Yes, I saw it."

"So someone took it while we were out."

The panic showed on my mum's face. "What if they're inside!"

Dad and I went to check every room. I looked behind doors and under beds, even opening the wardrobe to look inside. Next, Dad called the chief officer in the veterans' complex, and he treated the situation very seriously. Nothing like this had happened in the home before, he told my dad. They would post two soldiers by the building entrance for the rest of the night, to make sure whoever it was didn't return. It wasn't impossible, after all.

As we were getting ready to go to bed, Dad came into my son's room carrying a hefty walking stick in red wood with a dragon head handle. He put it by the head of the bed I was sleeping in. "Be on guard tonight," he warned. "In case anything happens." He then opened the top drawer in the chest of drawers and took out two large metal balls which he used for strengthening his hands, twizzling them around in his palm twice. They were for him to use if a situation arose.

"What do I use?" my son asked.

"You don't," said my dad. He's in his seventies now, doddering and podgy, and always sick with something, but for a moment he looked as fit as a fiddle again and ready for action. He was a soldier all his life – clearly his fighting instinct still kicked back in at the slightest whiff of a bad egg.

When he left the room, my son sat up on his bed, rocking his knees side to side. "Grandad looks nervous," he said.

"Old people are like that," I said.

The next morning, I was woken by the sound of talking in the living room. I opened my eyes and looked at the alarm clock on the bedside table. It was already past eight. My son was still dozing, snoring gently. I got up and dressed, went into the living room. Sat across from my parents were the complex chief and a police officer, listening to the full rundown of the night's events and the missing lock. I greeted the guests then went to clean my teeth and wash my face in the bathroom. I could hear Mum saying, "The corridor light broke two days ago as well. Do you think it's related?"

"Society is a mess," said the chief. "We have to be vigilant. I'll call a meeting today to discuss heightening security in the complex."

"From the looks of the door and what you're telling us, it doesn't sound like the work of your common thief. Taking the cylinder lock out wouldn't open the door," said the police officer.

My dad didn't sound convinced. "Then who was it? It's not that easy to pry the lock out of a door."

I was shaking my head as I brushed my teeth. This was all a little much for what had happened, I thought.

It was no more than a run-of-the-mill robbery attempt. The burglar thought there was no one in, but when they realised they were wrong, they scarpered. Simple. There was no need to pick over every little detail.

After our guests left, I went into the kitchen for some breakfast. I was going to eat and then pack before saying my goodbyes. My train was at eleven, so I had loads of time. Halfway through my breakfast, Mum crept into the kitchen really suspiciously and whispered,

"Follow me." I looked at her, confused, but went with her anyway into their bedroom where she pushed the door to, behind us.

"What's up?" I asked.

Dad was on the sofa, a serious look on his face. "It wasn't a burglar who took the lock."

"Oh, then who was it?"

Dad put his hand into his pocket and brought out a metal tubelike object which he held up to me. It was the lock. "I put my hand in my pocket a moment ago not really thinking, and found this. I checked it against the door already. It's ours."

"So what happened?" This was all very strange. "How did it end up in your pocket?" Before he answered, there was a moment when I started to imagine that the burglar had snuck into the house and dropped the lock into Dad's coat pocket before slipping away without anyone noticing. But why would anybody do that?

"There's only one explanation," said my dad. "It was one of us who removed the lock."

I blinked. I knew right away what he was implying. "That's impossible. Come on, now." Though I didn't really believe what I was saying.

"What else could it be?" said Mum. My dad was nodding earnestly.

I thought about it for a moment and agreed that they

had to be right. We discussed what to do about it. People already believed that there was a burglar. The chief had even come over, with a police officer! Management were notifying all the other residents as we spoke. How would we explain to them that we had found the lock, and it had been in one of our pockets all along?

"We let them believe it," I said. "Stick to the same story, say nothing else. And we definitely don't tell anyone that the lock was in Dad's pocket."

"That's all we can do," said Mum.

We left it with me making one final request of them both. "We put this whole thing to rest now, it's as far as it goes. It doesn't get brought up ever, not even at home. We act like it never happened. OK?"

They nodded.

I went into my son's bedroom and shut the door, then sat on the edge of his bed.

He wasn't stirring yet. I watched his features as he lay, deep in sleep. After a long moment, his eyelashes twitched, and his eyes opened. He looked like he had been awake a while, and there was an odd expression on his face. We stayed there, looking at each other, in silence, neither of us speaking.

Then I bent down and kissed his forehead and said quietly, "Baba is going soon."

My son reached his hand out from under the covers and gripped mine.

Neighbours

When Xu Liang's neighbours from across the hall moved house, they left a pile of rubbish outside the door.

The family had lived there for five or so years. The husband, somewhere in his forties, was tall and lanky, and wore glasses. The wife must have been a decade his junior, and even thinner than him, and a little shorter. She also had glasses. Together they had a sickly-looking eight-year-old son. Or maybe he was seven.

This was the most that Xu Liang knew about the family. He had no idea of their names, or what they did for work. He couldn't remember saying even one word to them the whole time they had lived across from him. If he ever bumped into them on his way in or out, he gave them a nod of the head, if anything at all, and more often than not they just walked past each other as if neither had noticed the other. If anyone had asked Xu Liang, he would have told them that the family, the boy included, were a little full of themselves, even arrogant. In other words, they were the types to prefer to keep people at the other end of a ten-foot pole. He got the impression that living in an old place like his block was, for them, sheer condescension, as if they had no choice in the matter. It was little surprise that none of the neighbours, nor Xu Liang, had been queueing up outside their door to make friends. Although, if anyone had asked them, it was unlikely they would have said that Xu Liang was all that normal either.

But really! A middle-aged man, with no wife or family to speak of, living in a flat alone. They probably thought the bachelor boy had something wrong with him, a mental illness, or was just plain odd. Why else wouldn't he have settled down yet? Of course, with exactly zero neighbourliness between them, there was never going to be anything more. Neither needed the other to get by.

So there is something funny in the fact that it was only after the family had moved out that Xu Liang finally, through no fault of his own, came to know a little about them.

The flats occupied by Xu Liang and his ex-neighbour were the only two on the top floor of the old building he called home.

After his neighbours left, Xu Liang would walk past the pile of rubbish in the hall whenever he was coming or going, and it would always make him feel uncomfortable. The two doors were fairly close together, only three metres apart, at most, so the rubbish was as much outside his flat as it was outside theirs.

Still, Xu Liang was determined to do nothing about it at first – it was not his mess to deal with, but before a week went by he couldn't take it any more. The rubbish pile was an eyesore. He had to get rid.

He fetched his dustpan and broom and went at the pile. Halfway through the job, underneath all the newspapers, he came across an empty medicine packet about the size of his palm, on which was written "Cervicitis balm". Xu Liang cocked his head and read the first word, then reread it, then reread it again. Deciding to investigate further, he bent down to pick up the packet and look over the instructions. But he stopped his hand hovering just above the packet. What if it was dirty? This was the thought that gave him pause. He didn't need the instructions to know the medicine's purpose, it was printed right there on the packet.

Except, the word for cervicitis usually had one more character in it: 宫颈炎, not only 宫炎. At least, that was what he had heard it being called before. Who had the cervicitis, anyway? There had been only one woman living across from him as far as he knew, with her husband and son. But could he say for sure? He had no idea even how serious the condition was or what cervicitis represented for a woman's health. Might this have explained her thinness? But then her husband was just as thin.

So if not that, then what? And how did she catch it? Poor hygiene? Risky sex? In Xu Liang's mind, a genteel woman like her would be on top of her hygiene. Daily showers, maybe. But if not, she at least washed her downstairs every day. And when it came to any pre-coital preparations, she couldn't have gone to bed without them, would demand them even. So what had happened? Perhaps only she and her husband knew.

Xu Liang pictured her then, her rail-thin figure and, when he moved his gaze down to her crotch, an inflamed organ that was even leaking pus. He felt like puking. The image was undoubtedly disgusting, but it couldn't overshadow his surprise at the discovery itself. And of course! A woman he had zero connection with had, by accident, allowed him a window into a secret illness inside of her. That's not the sort of thing you just find out on an average day. This was a woman's ultimate privacy.

But Xu Liang did not have to wait long before he made another discovery. This time it was about the man. A secret that affected Xu Liang just as much as the original one, if not a hell of a lot more, it shook up his quiet life.

The flat opposite had stayed empty since the move. Then, one lunchtime, Xu Liang heard the door to it being opened. He hurried up to his peephole to spy on who was outside. It was the man. The flat still belonged to them. Why, then, had he come back, alone? Were there things inside still needing to be taken away? Were they going to rent the place out and he was there to get it ready? Xu Liang didn't really fancy waiting around to find out. It was getting late and his bed was calling. Only then came a sound from the hallway, the click-clacking of heels against hard flooring. Xu Liang skidded back to his door and pressed his eye to the peephole. Sure enough, there was a woman, but this woman was certainly not the wife. From behind, she looked mid-height, curvy, and she had her hair clipped at the shoulders. He couldn't tell her age exactly, but her figure and clothing suggested she was no girl. She pushed open the unlocked door and slipped inside, then quickly shut it behind her.

No more than a dozen minutes went by, if that, and the moans started up. They were not wasting any time. Xu Liang hadn't known that a woman could be so noisy in bed. She could have been right next to him. He found himself in the sort of daze that follows a heavy blow. Slowing his breath to hear better, he could make out the clear rhythm of her moaning, like when there was a pause of a few seconds before they resumed. The sounds hadn't gone on for long, at least as far as Xu Liang's ears could tell, before there came a series of breathy, hurried phrases from the flat, followed by an ecstatic scream. Then silence.

Xu Liang waited with bated breath for any more sounds. When he heard the door opening again, he jumped out of bed and, forgetting his slippers, scuttled over to the peephole. He was too late. The hallway was empty but for that same click-clacking of high-heeled footsteps echoing up the staircase. He was just settling back into bed when he heard the door once more. The man was leaving.

* * *

Every week after this, on one afternoon, except Saturdays and Sundays, the man and woman would return. One afternoon, every week.

It was always the same order of events, the pair arriving and leaving separately.

This didn't explain much besides them being careful planners who didn't want to make their activities public. So no one would make any unwelcome connections. But Xu Liang also found it surprising just how consistent every stage was in the whole affair, not simply the order of their arrival and departure, but of every beat, from her slipping in the door, to the moaning, to the cry of ecstasy and beyond. It was as if they had calculated every minute and wouldn't permit a slip of even a handful of seconds either way. Xu Liang would sit there forecasting what stage was up next. Here come the big moans, he'd think to himself, and sure enough, they came. She's leaving now, he mused, and click, the door across the hall opened, and click clack, click clack, the woman strutted away.

Where's the variety? Xu Liang wondered.

They could chat a little first, maybe, flirt a while, try some foreplay. They didn't need to do it the moment they were in the door. Afterwards they could lie on the bed together, share with each other the parts about it they liked, what they're grateful for, or else talk up the other's sexual prowess, that never goes amiss. Must they hop out of bed as quick as they hopped in? They were like animals. Xu Liang suspected that the reason they were so monotone and mechanical, so set in their ways, had a lot to do with the man. Without a doubt that louse had zero notion of intimacy or romance. Just one look at the self-absorbed loser told a person all they needed to know: the guy lacked heart and was only out for himself. All he wanted was physical satisfaction. The woman was probably different. Her passionate performance in the bedroom was enough to show that she was a real vixen, an enchantress.

A woman like her wasn't going to be satisfied with just a shag, she had other needs, of this Xu Liang had no doubt. So who was this guy's lover? Xu Liang supposed they were colleagues, and he her line manager. He was taking advantage, pulling rank to pull her. She had little choice but to submit. This kind of thing happened all the time. It was a shame. Xu Liang genuinely pitied her.

While this was all going on, Xu Liang noticed that, in contrast to the pair's set routine, certain small changes were happening in his own life.

First, his daily midday nap was now interrupted once a week. And not simply interrupted. On more than one occasion he had climbed out of bed and stood waiting by the peephole for the woman to leave the opposite flat so he could get a look at her face. He never managed to. She always left with her head down and, as if by design, the two sides of her fringe covering her features. Like she knew full well, already, that there was someone pinned to the other side of the neighbour's door desperate to clock her. She was no doubt a shy girl. Which both disappointed Xu Liang and delighted him. The disappointment came from not being able to see her face, the delight from the fact that so many modern women turned his stomach with their brash, flamboyant behaviour, like the only way they could advertise their charm was to bare teeth and claws. Xu Liang still firmly believed that a woman should be gentle and reticent. Explosive passion, yes, that was good too, it was necessary even, but there was a time and a place for it, in private, in the bedroom. In company, a woman ought to be a paragon of virtue and restraint. This was nothing to do with artifice, it was about the genuine issue that a woman should seem like a woman. Anyone who believes they're not faking something should take a lap of their neighbourhood in their birthday suit and prove it.

Listening to the woman's footsteps on the staircase, Xu Liang asked himself what she was like. Her clothing didn't stand out, but it was well put together. A forest green coat, form-fitting, ever so slightly accentuated her chest. Her jeans were straight leg. Her hair had been pressed then curled slightly inwards at the ends. Her person seemed wholly unremarkable. But Xu Liang knew that under this unremarkable exterior was hiding a spirit that blazed red hot. Did she have a husband? Were they happy? Might she have divorced?

When Xu Liang could no longer hear her descending footsteps, he had more than once been struck with the urge to open his door and rush after her. He wanted to follow her, see where she worked, where she lived, then through some roundabout means or tedious connection meet her. It wasn't completely unfeasible, right? He only had to meet her and he would then be able to know her. He would be open, honest with her, tell her the type of person he was, his experiences, his real opinion of women. He would recount his failed marriage, and how a matchmaking agency set him up with others, only for him to sit through one unsuccessful date after another. His story would move her. He would find a way to make her leave that pretentious arse and become *his* lover. That way he wouldn't only hear that soul-stirring moaning, he would feel it, which would undoubtedly be all the more marvellous. Only, was any of this feasible? Because once he had calmed down and was thinking it out loud, it all started to seem so ridiculous.

The second change that happened for Xu Liang was how much more sleep he started to lose at night. Lying in bed, tossing and turning, he fretted and groaned. Some thoughts he simply couldn't shake off. This had never happened to him before. He thought about sleeping pills. But he decided they were only a last resort, it was better not to take them. Once he started, he might not be able to stop.

For now, whenever he felt himself struggling to sleep, his only strategy was to stay in bed and watch TV until exhaustion took hold.

* * *

On one restless night, he flicked on the telly and clicked between channels for something that might keep his attention a while. The show that jumped out at him was a documentary of sorts on the local sights and scenery. Xu Liang liked this type of programme better than the vapid, interminable dramas. The narrator was talking about Oxhead Mountain. On screen there were these great sweeping shots of the landscape. Xu Liang had been there once, as a kid, on a school trip in the spring if he remembered rightly. That was years ago, and he had no recollection of the place now, so he felt like he was seeing it for the first time. The area was a wealth of gently sloping rises and stretches of green meadow and bright flowers. At the mountain's foot was a lake, smallish, sunlight dancing across its surface, and beside it a wood-and-straw pavilion. There were verdant trees, stone slab pathways, streams, a temple, a pagoda. It was nothing if not pleasing to the eye.

Heading deeper into the mountains, the frame settled on a massive cliff face where some carved writing could be seen. The camera zoomed in slowly, giving every single character that was engraved into the rock its clear moment in the frame. One carving, in particular, and the voiceover that accompanied it, caught Xu Liang's attention. It read:

Uncle brought my cousin and me for a spring walk on Oxhead Mountain
This is so we remember Xiao Yun, of Mafu Street
Spring of the 53rd Year Under the Qianlong Emperor

Xu Liang sat upright in bed. He lived on Mafu Street. The Xiao Yun who had left that note in the rock had lived there once too. Mafu Street was a classic lane, short and narrow, so regardless of precisely where Xiao Yun had lived back then, her home couldn't have been all that far from Xu Liang's place. They were as good as neighbours. Only, they were neighbours separated by two hundred-odd years. Reading this note left more than two centuries ago, carved in rock, felt almost like a miracle to him.

Xu Liang pictured that neighbour now, the little girl from two hundred years earlier, strolling across the meadow. That was a spring of long grass and warblers in flight, and this young girl called Xiao Yun, side-by-side with her cousin, was following her uncle along the mountain pass. Xiao Yun and her cousin were definitely the best of friends growing up, then as that first simmering of attraction for the opposite sex surfaced, they would come to admire each other, and in time receive the blessing of their parents. But even so, in that distant past, it wasn't proper for young men and young women to be alone together, and the pair had to be accompanied by an elder family member for this trip to the mountain. Just imagine them, the frolicking, happy young couple from the Qing dynasty, their clothes flapping in the wind, capering around this beautiful mountain valley, their caring elder not far behind.

That night was a better night for Xu Liang than he had for ages, spent being carried along by these warm thoughts, before drifting, gradually, into dreamland.

Pock

Forty-five was a lucky age for Pock. He couldn't have been more thankful. He had always remembered a line the Monkey King had said in an opera highlight he watched as a child: "Everyone has their turn as emperor, next year it's mine." As far as Pock was concerned, this stroke of luck was as good as a stint on the throne.

In hindsight Pock saw there had been signs, his very own auspicious clouds like the ones that appear before a royal birth. Good omen number one came when he lost his goose. His only goose. This reared bird was the only living creature in his home, besides himself. But the bird had gone, and he had searched high and low for it, checking the village's outskirts and all the nearby ditches and streams. But in the end, he trudged home empty-handed and spent the rest of the day gazing despondently at a splatter of goose muck.

That same night, he had a dream. He saw his widowed mother, who had been dead for years already. She was lying on the funeral slab, a candle lit next to her head to guide her spirit onward, and a fine, snow white silk draped over her body. A peaceful expression on her fair face, she was in much better shape than in his horrid memory of her. He knelt at her side, the ceremonial stick he had to carry as her son laid across his palms, and bowed.

"Ma," he said, "please help your son find his goose. Ma, help me find that goose." It was just as he was begging his ma like this that her throat started to gurgle like she was choking on phlegm, and Pock almost jumped out of bed in fright. But when he woke in the morning and went to open his door, who would waddle straight in but the goose.

The second omen came at the start of the month. He went into town to sell his dried chilli peppers and had emptied the two buckets by midday. While he was on his way to pick up a baked sesame bun to tide him over until dinner, a wave of hunger hit that sent him hurrying towards the nearby restaurant, The Drunk Scholar, where he ordered portions of simmered pork liver and stir-fried pork and celery, plus a bottle of fifty-five proof vintage Fenjin Pavilion to wash down the food. He ate his fill and got a little carried away with the drink, and when he was ready for home, he struggled to his feet and tottered out.

There were seven or so miles between the town and his village. Bare-chested and carrying the shoulder yoke with its empty buckets dangling at either end, he followed a trail along the embankments of a paddy field. But the booze quickly got the better of him. His head started spinning and, a few steps later, he dropped the pole and keeled over, straight into a pond. Under the glaring sun, the water's surface shone a blinding white.

A toad, disturbed by Pock sploshing into the shallow water only a foot from where it had been resting, hopped away and a little up the bank, then turned to face the intruder, looking him up and down with an expression like confusion at the pockmarked face he confronted: is this fella a giant version of me? There it sat, staring and unmoving, apparently having made up its mind to get to the bottom of this stranger. Pock stared back, and as he looked into the toad's eyes, he thought he sensed warmth there, the kind of warmth he had only ever found in a woman's eyes. He rolled onto his side, slipped a hand into his trousers and, taking himself in his grip, started to tug. The toad edged away. Pock threw up. He had felt his stomach churn, then up came every last drop of his lunch. Feeling groggy, he slumped where he sat and drifted off.

It was dusk when he came to. Bats crowded the washed-out blue overhead, and in the distance, a thread of smoke wound skywards. It took a moment for him to remember where he was. He shuffled his body around so he could start to stand up, and then froze; positioned around him were six softshell turtles of various sizes. At first, he thought the turtles might have come to eat him while he was asleep, but when he looked again, he saw they were laid flat, as still as the dead, in the pool of his rejected lunch. They must have smelled the meal he had so unceremoniously ejected all over their home, and made their way up from the pond's bottom to take advantage of the free feast, only to end up drunk and poisoned from the undigested alcohol. Seeing an opportunity, Pock scooped the turtles into his buckets, then headed back to town as fast as his feet would carry him.

There, he sold the lot for the price of three hundred yuan a kilo, and suddenly found himself seven hundred odd yuan richer. Such a big wad of notes for so little trouble, it was enough to make Pock forget himself for a moment, and he started to figure that if he could get his hands on just a little more money, he might be able to find himself a wife. That thought alone was enough to stir up the remaining booze in his body, and soon had him mooning over the prospect.

* * *

He had missed his chance a long while before. Whether that was ten or twelve years ago, he couldn't remember. He had done with work for the day and decided to take the scenic route home, pickaxe on his shoulder, via the abandoned kilns by the riverside.

Pock often went there when he had nothing on. He liked to climb the kilns and spy on the women squatting along the river washing clothes. Their bottoms in the air, sleeves rolled up to their armpits, was a scene that stoked the bolder reaches of Pock's imagination. He'd sometimes picture what it would be like if one of them was his wife, cleaning his stinking clothes for him so he didn't have to.

She'd finish scrubbing them, then head home, washing basket under her arm, where she would say to Pock, "Dinner's ready in the pot, can't you open the thing yourself?"

"I was waiting for you, to eat together," Pock would reply.

"What's there worth waiting for?" she'd say, giving a moue.

"A person can't eat alone, it makes the tummy uneasy," Pock would chuckle. Then the pair would enjoy dinner together, before going to bed... The mere thought had him reaching inside his pants. But on this occasion, Pock didn't have to imagine. He threw down his pickaxe and was about to start scrambling up the kiln when he noticed, half hidden in the kiln entrance, a woman. Her hair messy and matted, she wore a filthy black rag, tied at the waist with cord, and her bare feet were caked in mud.

She looked like she was maybe in her forties. Straw clung to her face, and there was a bowl in the dirt next to her. Pock edged closer, and hearing him, the woman's head spun around to look. When she saw it was a man, she reached out a grey, wizened hand and croaked, in an unfamiliar accent, "Mister, some coins?"

"I don't have any," Pock said.

"Money, sir," she continued, as if she hadn't heard, still reaching towards him.

Pock turned out his pockets. "Look, nothing."

The woman dropped her hand to her side and fell quiet. Pock took a few more steps around her, then glanced about him, and finally sat down next to her.

"You're also looking for food?" the woman asked.

Pock looked down at his clothing and questioned for a moment whether he wasn't a beggar just like her.

"I'm not begging," he said. "I have food. I grow it. It's money I don't have."

"You have food. That's good."

"It's better than being hungry."

"Mister has a good life."

"Good life, my arse." Pock spat a great glob of saliva onto the dirt.

"But you have food to eat."

"It's true, and it's better than going hungry."

"Is that your village, over there?"

"Right."

"Mister's a good person. You'll feed me, won't you?"

"Wait a while, and then we'll go."

Pock waited until it was dark before telling the woman to follow him home. When they reached the village, they snuck along the streets, sticking close to walls and slipping around corners, until they were inside, where Pock dropped straight into a seat and told the woman, "Get cooking." So she did. When the food was ready, Pock said, "Bring it over." So the woman filled a bowl and carried it across the room to him. When they were both done eating, the woman tidied away the bowls and chopsticks, then Pock said, "Wash my feet."

The woman slept on the pile of hay in the kitchen corner that night. Pock made her leave before first light. He was afraid someone would see. He still had big dreams of marriage back then. But a neighbour, who had awoken early to shovel the village shit, spotted her. In no time, the village was abuzz with the rumour that Pock and the beggar woman had done it. They hadn't, though. Not that "it" hadn't been his plan to start with, but for whatever reason they just hadn't. Pock felt robbed.

A few years before then, as a fresh thirty-year-old,

Pock had gone to have his fortune told by a monk at the local temple. The monk had reeled off all of these mystical-sounding proclamations while staring off at seemingly nothing, with eyes glazed, and the whole time Pock had sat there tapping his foot impatiently until he couldn't take it any more and fixed the monk with a stern look.

"Marriage. Marriage. Tell me about my marriage."

The monk looked over Pock's face for what felt like an age, then weighing his words carefully, said, "A pockmarked and ruddy face is a sure sign of good fortune in future. Your broad brow and thin eyebrows mean your luck will come from the southeast."

"Yes, and? What else?"

The monk shook his head. "Heaven's will shall not be revealed."

"When did me finding myself a woman become Heaven's will?"

"All is as Heaven wills it."

Pock thought a lot about what the monk had said. The Xu clan village was to the southeast, surrounded by a dyke. Could that be where he would find his future betrothed? Pock asked if someone headed that way could do some enquiring for him, and it turned out there really was a woman in the village who would fit him just right: a hunchback. But the hunchback was already promised to a cripple, and the wedding was to be in a few days. There was nothing Pock could do. So he set to thinking further afield. Southeast of the Xu clan village was the county town, but a town girl wouldn't give him a second look, he knew that. Pock had been tricked, he realised. "That bloody bald donkey," he cursed.

But how hadn't he thought of his own plot? That was in the village's southeast corner. And it was there that, dozens of years later, Pock's luck would finally turn around. By then, he had long put all those dreams of matrimony behind him. But women also want things – he hadn't considered that before.

The big day was now embedded deep in Pock's memory. A flash or detail only had to come to mind for him to become as excited again as on the day itself.

He had eaten lunch and headed home in a hurry. He had a drainage ditch to dig. In the baking heat of the afternoon sun, all was quiet but for the monotonous chirring of the cicadas. He dug for a while and was soon dripping with sweat. He threw aside his shirt and sat bare-chested beneath a willow at the field's edge to rest. He was starting to doze off when the wife of Fucai, the carpenter who owned the next field over, stepped out from between two rows of string bean plants. She was wearing a pink shirt that stopped at her waist and was carrying a basket half full of string beans.

"Pock, what are you doing?" she asked.

"Doing? Nothing much. Digging a ditch. Where's Fucai?"

"He went across the river first thing. There's a family in Hexi Village wanting some furniture." Fucai's wife kept on speaking as she approached the willow and sat down not far from Pock.

She was thirty-something and dumpy, with wide hips and a large chest, and she blinked constantly when she spoke, like the words came out of her eyes.

"The sun's still high," she said, blinking. "Why aren't you tucked up asleep? Digging a ditch at this time of day?"

"I can't sleep. It's too warm."

"It's not 'cause you're warm," Fucai's wife sniggered, showing a set of yellowed teeth. "I figure you've got no hole in your bed that you can dig, so you've got to come out to here dig one instead."

Pock thought she was acting strange. She had said some salty things before, but only ever when there were others around, working the fields.

"Fucai is a lucky man," Pock said. "There's a hole in his bed."

"He should think himself lucky, for sure. Only, he can't dig that hole."

Pock didn't respond. He was thinking about how old the carpenter was. Forty-five, the same as him. What was the man's problem? Pock thought he would have no issue in that department. As long as he was eating well, he could still squeeze one out occasionally.

Plucking up courage, Pock said, "Fucai–"

"Turn around."

"Why?"

"I need to pee."

Pock looked away. He thought she would go between the rows of string beans, but it didn't sound like she walked away. Then he heard a stream of liquid hit the ground somewhere behind him. He held his breath and listened. It was like music to his ears. When it stopped, Pock turned back around. He found Fucai's wife with her trousers still around her knees. Somehow, they had become stuck and wouldn't come up. Straight away, Pock's eyes became glued to the dark patch between her legs. He blocked out everything else. How long had Pock lived without ever seeing such a thing before? He couldn't control himself, and like a hungry tiger he pounced.

Pock pinched his own leg when he was finished. Ow! So I'm not dreaming, he thought.

"What stinks on you?" Fucai's wife's question was further proof it wasn't a dream.

She was blinking as she asked it, but this time as if she was trying to discern what exactly had just happened.

Pock spent whole days after in a daze. He could get

nothing done. In his head, he had constant replays of those amorous moments going round and round. Shame that was all he had to take away. His luck had come and gone like a ripple in a breeze. That day also marked a change in his carpenter neighbour, Fucai. The man had once been unable to spend more than a few days cooped up at home before he would be desperate to be off somewhere for work, and sometimes he was away for a week or two. But now he was like a nesting hen.

The day after Pock's little victory, he had done as any man would do and ran straight to the carpenter's house, where he loitered around outside until Fucai's wife appeared. When she came out carrying a basket of dirty clothes, Pock followed her. He waited until the village boundary before hurrying to catch up and said, in a hushed voice, "Where were you? Come on, let's go to the field."

Fucai's wife didn't turn around. "Can't. The old man's here. He'll kill me if he finds out."

"So what?" said an exasperated Pock. "It's just a couple of minutes."

"No. I said no, and I mean no. Ask me when he's gone to work again."

"When will that be?"

"How would I know?"

"I don't think I can wait."

"Had enough of life, then?"

No, he hadn't, not nearly enough. In fact, he felt like his life was just getting started. He was about to tell Fucai's wife just that when she quickened her pace and left him watching her go, as she shouted a hello to a passing woman. Pock could do nothing but stand there in a huff as she disappeared out of sight.

But the day eventually came when Fucai went off for work again, with Pock hoping against hope that he never returned. No sooner had the carpenter stepped off his property than Pock went sidling up to the house and in through the door. Fucai's wife was the only one in since the children had gone to school. She was sitting on the bed mending clothes.

"Fucai's gone," he said, his voice shaking. "I saw him leave."

She glanced up and her expression immediately turned to shock. "What are you doing in my home? Did anyone see you?" She blinked at him.

"No, no," said Pock, waving his hands in front of him anxiously. "I was careful."

"Well, get out."

"You too. Come to the field with me."

"What field, I'm not a dog."

"Then where?" Pock looked at her, confused. "Fucai's gone, you said–"

"I'll come to you when it's dark. Now go. My ma will be back anytime now."

"OK, mine, tonight. No tricking me, OK."

"Go!" She threw the clothing she was holding in his face.

Pock went straight to town. He had remembered what Fucai's wife had said that day, in the fields, about his stink. He wanted to buy some nice-smelling soap and have a good wash. He tried two shops and looked at all of the options available before finally settling on one with a package that had the image of a woman on it.

It was a foreign woman, who Pock thought looked a little like Fucai's wife.

The rest of the afternoon he spent sitting in the doorway of his home waiting for dark.

He felt like a lifetime had passed before the light at last started to fade.

He ate dinner, then heated a pot of water to a steady bubble and sat down in his wooden tub and washed himself with the new soap. He did so with more care than ever before, making sure he didn't miss a spot. It reminded him of the scene when his mother had died, of washing her body on his own because there was no other family to help. He had been equally careful on that occasion too.

"Ma," he mumbled. "Your son's life is good now..."

When he felt clean, he patted himself dry, then climbed onto the bed as naked as the day he was born.

He lay there for a full two hours.

She never showed.

It got to the point, eventually, when Pock dressed again and went out. Most of the houses in the village were dark by that time. Everyone was sleeping. Everywhere was quiet. The only sounds were Pock's footsteps and the nearby dogs' barks caused by those footsteps.

There were lights on in Fucai's home. Pock crept up to the side of the building and, standing on a broken basket so he could reach the window, peered inside. Fucai and his wife were sat under the covers talking. She was laughing at something he had just said.

"That fucking bint." Pock stepped off the basket and paused for a few minutes, under the windowsill. He then went around to the front and tried the kitchen door. It was open. He went in. This was where the first spark was ignited.

Floozy

"Our family raised a floozy," said Mother.

She meant once upon a time, of course. She would have struggled to say anything with conviction about the present day. She was getting on in age. When our life nears its end, we find comfort in reminiscing about the past.

"She would have been your aunt," said Mother. "She wasn't even twenty when she died."

Mother was almost seventy now.

* * *

Your grandfather never forgave your aunt, said Mother, even after her death. The mourning room was set up in the second hall, and your grandfather made sure never to look in that direction, as if he had no idea of what was inside. The body was wrapped in the finest snowy silk, laid on a slab, the face waxen yellow against the white, and the mouth sagging at the corners as though in remorse at the thought of the debauched life she had led. Your uncle, her husband, was devastated, but all he could do was kneel in the mourning room sobbing quietly into his hands. The day of the funeral, Grandmother sent a servant, trembling, to tell Grandfather, "Sir, your daughter-in-law is being carried out."

Grandfather sat with his opium pipe laid across his palms in a mahogany armchair, its armrests burnished by use. He had his eyes shut, as if he was sleeping.

"Sir... Sir, it's time for your daughter-in-law to go." The thought of waking him only made the servant nervier.

Grandfather opened an eye and, a long moment later, grunted to show he had heard. Right on cue, the sound of wind instruments and drumming started up outside the main gate.

Your aunt's father and my father used to be schoolmates, and were good friends. They sat the imperial exam together and stayed overnight at the same inn to break up the journey. They talked through the night and, in an excited moment, swore that from then on they would be family.

Grandfather's town held a great celebration for him every time he set off for another exam. One of the ceremonies involved having the servant designated to travel with him squat down and then take the shoulder yoke, laden with their luggage, while people crowded around jeering and teasing. "Can he lift it?" they asked aloud. "Will he lift it?"

The servant would put on that he was struggling and then slowly rise until at a certain height he shot up ramrod straight with a single jolt, the yoke still balanced on his shoulders. Everyone would cheer, "He's done it!" and, "He managed this time!" and, "Who'd have guessed!"

But Grandfather didn't deliver the same success. He failed one exam after another, and in the end he never managed to jump to his feet, so to speak. He resigned himself instead to settling down early and raising a family. Your aunt's father, meanwhile, was a rising star. He passed every exam he sat and eventually became a high official.

When Grandmother was pregnant with her third child, your aunt's mother had just become pregnant with her first. This was because her husband, Grandfather's friend, delayed their marriage on account of his official duties. The promise that the two friends had made during their trip all those years before could now be kept. The newborns were a boy and a girl.

When they were both six years old, the official marriage proposals were exchanged but the betrothed did not meet again until the wedding. In the meantime, rumours circulated that Uncle's wife-to-be had a face riddled with pockmarks, and she was blind in one eye. The rumours had likely been started in response to how tall and handsome Uncle had grown to be, on top of the fact that he came from good stock. The thought of his marrying someone deformed was probably a comfort to any jealous local. But this was a time when life was a spare affair, and villagers told tall tales to entertain themselves. Whatever the reason, your aunt who had not once stepped out of her family home was considered by all in the village to be unfortunate-looking. But Uncle never complained.

Of course, had he objected, it would not have done any good – a marriage arranged was not so easily changed. And at least rumour had not yet gone so far as to call your aunt a monkey. He had to trust fate.

But just in case, come their wedding night, Uncle chose not to bolt the door of the nuptial chamber, as it would make for an easier escape if the rumours turned out to be true. Though this did allow one of the eaves-droppers at the door to stick their head inside at one point. But nobody could make a man share a room with his new wife even if he did not wish it, not even Grandfather. His hands trembling, Uncle hesitated before he removed her red veil. He discovered that rather than blind or pockmarked, his young wife had blossomed into an exceptionally charming woman. This was better than any great windfall. On seeing Uncle, Aunt was also relieved. Later, she would tell him that while she was cooped up in her parents' home, people had often said she was to marry a hunchback, who even at his most upright stood no taller than a stove. They teased her that if her husband ever wanted to hit her, she would have to lift him up so he could reach her face. More idle hearsay.

The newlyweds quickly became very fond of each other and couldn't bear to spend a moment apart, even if they had to, Grandfather having set a rule that his daughter-in-law must cook and keep up the house with the servants. Grandfather occasionally ordered your uncle to go rent-collecting too, at which times Aunt would feel restless. On the days he was set to return home, she would limp along on her bound feet to the edge of the village to watch him coming, or quietly ask the servants to check when he would arrive. When he stepped through the door, she would rush to him in a flurry and shuffle about, waiting until her father-in-law was absent so she could talk with him freely. When Uncle had finished reporting the accounts to his father and was dismissed to get some rest, he would follow Aunt to their room in the rear wing.

A short time afterwards, Aunt became pregnant, and her body's response was intense. She would throw up whatever she ate, and having grown so used to being coddled in her childhood, this new suffering laid her low in bed, too weak to rise.

Uncle made an urgent trip into town to ask for the doctor to hurry over. He prepared all her medicinal broths himself, and when he wasn't otherwise engaged, he sat by his wife's bedside.

Ever since Uncle had married, his father had been leaving ever more of the family's business to your father and your two uncles to manage, though they had to provide regular and timely reports. In his newfound free time, Grandfather took on the task of teaching the younger children in the family and village. He saw reading and study as vital endeavours. During his lessons, everyone elsewhere in the home had to remain quiet, and the area around the study was out of bounds, unless anyone fancied finding themselves on the receiving end of Grandfather's temper. So at these times, the house seemed empty.

One day, Grandfather was holding his usual morning class in the study. He was sitting in his Taishi armchair, a thread-bound book open in his hand and his pipe resting on his leg ready to serve as pointer, if needed. Sat facing him was a class of wide-eyed and well-behaved children. Grandfather drew out the tones of each syllable as he read, "Among family, give of what one has to those in need. Respect should prevail between elders and youngsters, within and without the home. To listen to one's wife over one's flesh and blood is unbecoming of a man. To prioritise the material over the filial is unbefitting of a son. In marrying off a daughter, seek a worthy son-in-law without demanding excessive dowries. In taking a daughter-in-law, prioritise virtue. It is most shameful to flatter the rich and powerful. It is the height of ignominy to meet poverty with arrogance. Avoid disputes around the household, for they only lead to ruin. Exercise restraint in speech in all affairs, for excessive speech will only lead to error."

Grandfather read up to this point and then stopped, as though something had occurred to him. He put the book down and instructed the children to start memorising the passage. He stepped outside and shouted to his wife from under the eaves. When there was no reply, he crossed through the main hall, pipe still in hand, and went into the back rooms.

Having looked in several rooms and found no sign of Grandmother, he arrived at the door of Uncle's room and heard hushed conversation coming from the other side. He paused a moment, then used the pipe to nudge the door open.

An unsightly scene lay before him: your uncle was lying on the Ningbo bed, leant against the engraved railing, and reading a book; Aunt, her hair untied and splayed over Uncle's thigh where she rested her head, was listening to him read, her bare arm wrapped loosely around his waist. The pair looked up and saw Grandfather frozen in the doorway, the colour draining from his face. He turned and left.

Trembling, he barged into the kitchen. There he found me and your middle aunt and a number of women servants busy at work. Two recently culled hens lay on the stovetop, their heads resting at unlikely angles. Several tea kettles were warming on top of the large brazier in the centre of the room and spurting wisps of steam – positioned so in case Grandfather wanted a drink. He approached the brazier and stood there, silent. No one had noticed his entrance, which no doubt only made your grandfather crosser.

He drew back a leg and gave the brazier a ferocious kick, sending it tumbling to the ground. There was an almighty crash like a mountain being rent in two, and ash and water were sent flying up to the rafters.

There was shouting, dogs barking. A moment later, Grandmother, your father and middle uncle, along with a scramble of other family members and servants, young and old, ran in. With all this going on around him, Grandfather stood as stiff as a statue, his face caked with ash and dust like a forgotten idol.

No one dared step forward apart from

Grandmother, who edged closer and tugged at his sleeve. “Grandfather, my love, what is it?”

His expression was blank.

“Tell us, my love, what is it?”

For a moment it seemed like he wouldn’t reply and then his body started to shake again, the ash and dust coming off him like he was a long-resting bodhisattva risen anew. Suddenly he bellowed, “Kill her... I’ll kill... I’ll kill her... this... this... this home... is no... no... no brothel!”

* * *

Mother aped Grandfather’s cursing in her telling, then broke into laughter.

“Grandfather had a stammer,” she said. “The angrier he was, the worse it got.”

“That must be where I get my stammer from,” I said.

“Exactly,” she replied. “Your great-grandfather passed his stammer to my dad, and he to your uncle, but not to me. It’s only the men in the family who stammer. Both you and your brother have a bit of one. I’ve also noticed your son’s speech is a little clumsy.”

That got me thinking. People’s cultural backgrounds and their customs and values all change over time, but our ailments can pass down the generations. A hundred, maybe even a thousand or ten thousand years later, when each of us has turned to dust and scattered in the wind, what ails us will persist, and in their own way it is these traits that will carry us into perpetuity.

* * *

Continuing with the story, Mother explained that Grandmother had noticed something and called for Father and Middle Uncle to take Grandfather to his room to rest. Grandmother then instructed the others to tidy the mess in the kitchen before she went off to find Uncle and Aunt.

In the meantime, Uncle, knowing that such a severe transgression wouldn't be easily forgiven, had climbed the old pagoda tree in the rear courtyard, hopped over the wall and run away. He left his wife behind, trembling on the bed, having wet herself. When Grandmother entered, she started to cry.

"What is it?" Grandmother asked in a quiet voice, closing the door behind her.

"We... we..." Through snot and tears, and in fits and starts, Aunt slowly relayed what had happened.

"You have no sense of propriety, either of you," said Grandmother, sighing. She comforted Aunt for a while before asking for Mother to be brought to sit in her stead, in case Aunt did something stupid. She also called for several servants to go and search for Uncle, in case he did something stupid. This was a serious matter, so the concern was well justified.

Grandfather was so irate he didn't eat for two days. During those two days, Grandmother moped, fed up with the tongue-lashings she received when trying to wait on her husband. She understood his reaction, she knew the importance of decorum, of appearances, and she could not make up for her loved ones' error, so naturally there was nothing she could say.

Aunt tried on several occasions to rise from bed so she could throw herself at Grandfather's feet and bow and scrape, admit her wrongdoing and beg for punishment, but she was stopped every time by Mother. Grandfather was at the peak of his anger, Mother told her. He would calm down soon enough and eventually come around.

It wasn't until late on that fateful day that the servants who had gone in search of Uncle finally returned and furtively reported to Grandmother that they hadn't found him. There was no sign of him in any nearby lakes or rivers either, so presumably he had not yet done anything drastic. Later they would learn that, afraid his father was going to break his legs, he had run the dozens of miles to Tongcheng County Town where he used a pseudonym to find work in a shop. A whole six months of late nights and early mornings later, he had taken what he could of the hardship. Uncle would tell stories of his time at the shop for years afterwards, a trace of pride in his voice. It was something to be proud of, after all: he was the only family member in generations who had put himself to such hard physical labour.

This experience would prove lifesaving in the years to come. Your father, who had never really known hunger before, died of oedema following three years of penury post-Liberation. Your middle uncle withstood only a few kicks and punches from the Red Guards before his heart gave out. Whereas Uncle, who endured hard times aplenty, lived until a ripe old age, hale and hearty. He died only three years ago.

While still at the shop, he had someone deliver a letter to Grandmother so she knew he was safe. Several days later, Grandmother instructed her staff to carry Aunt in a sedan chair to Hetaozhuang where she would stay with Grandfather's youngest brother for a time. Uncle joined her six months later.

Back then, Grandfather's middle brother was running a timber business in Anqing, and his second youngest brother was the chair of the chamber of commerce in Shuangliu Town. The two of them, along with other members of the clan whose counsel Grandfather might heed, took it upon themselves to travel to our family home to persuade Grandfather that he should reconsider his stance, put the mistake down to naivety and forgive the couple. Grandfather only repeated that same line: "I'll kill... kill... I'll kill the girl..."

From then until Aunt's death, no one dared mention Uncle or her in front of Grandfather. It was as if they had never existed as part of the family. Only Grandmother, like a burglar in the night, would secretly order servants to check on the couple and deliver them supplies to her brother-in-law's home.

Then, after the reunion dinner one Mid-Autumn Festival evening, Grandfather turned to face Grandmother. "The boy's child will be due soon, I suppose," he said casually.

Grandmother was taken aback. "That's right, soon," she replied. "Darling, are you..."

She would have finished, but Grandfather's eyes had already closed.

Aunt died during the birth. The baby was too large and would not come despite three days and nights of pushing. In the end, the midwife had to pull out both child and womb together.

As she grew weaker, Aunt became delirious and started shouting, "Home... I want to go home... I want to go home..."

Uncle, with tears in his eyes, had had to lie, "You're already home. This is your home."

Aunt looked at Uncle as if she couldn't recognise him any more. Or maybe relations between husband

and wife had reached a point where love was no longer important to her. She went on shouting, "Home! Home!"

Sobbing, Grandmother stroked Aunt's bloodless cheeks. "You're home, child."

Aunt calmed down, perhaps believing Grandmother's words, and her lips formed a faint smile. She moved her head to regard Uncle and Grandmother and then, beyond, as if imagining that Grandfather was also standing there. The light in her eyes grew dim, and she spoke her final words: "Forgive me, I'm not a bad woman."

* * *

When Mother finished telling my aunt's story, she sat back in the sofa and shut her eyes, as though tired or in pain. I sensed her age then. She had been a good wife and a good mother all of her life, and she wouldn't be with us much longer. In the next world, maybe she would meet Aunt again, her young sister-in-law who died too soon labelled a "floozy". Maybe they would reminisce about better times. And if they did, what would they think of first?

About the Author

Gu Qian was born in 1958 in Tongcheng, Anhui Province. He started writing in the 1980s, publishing his first short story in 1985 having worked in various jobs including as a labourer, beekeeper, advertising sales manager and magazine editor. At the age of forty, he quit his job to write full-time, also starting a newspaper column. His published works include the short story collections *Flat Out*, *Hi, Long Time No See*, *A Woman's Details* and *Mutual Strangers*, and the novels *Go Elsewhere* and *Civilian Life*. His works have been included in many literary anthologies, and he has won the Zijin Mountain Literature Prize, the Jinling Literature Prize and the Nanjing Literature and Art Award. He lives in Nanjing, Jiangsu Province.

About the Translator

Jack Hargreaves is a translator of Yorkshire extraction. His literary work, recognised by English PEN and PEN America, includes the full-length works *Winter Pasture* by Li Juan and *Seeing* by Chai Jing, both co-translated with Yan Yan (Astra House); *Wait and See* by Zhu Hui, co-translated with Jun Liu (Phoenix Publishing, 2024); and *A Submarine in the Night* by Chen Chuncheng (Honford Star/Riverhead Books, 2025). He writes for the *China Books Review*.

ABOUT **SINO**IST BOOKS

We hope you enjoyed these stories about the exploits of a group of friends in Nanjing.

SINOIST BOOKS brings the best of Chinese fiction to English-speaking readers. We aim to create a greater understanding of Chinese culture and society, and provide an outlet for the ideas and creativity of the country's most talented authors.

To let us know what you thought of this book, or to learn more about the diverse range of exciting Chinese fiction in translation we publish, find us online. If you're as passionate about Chinese literature as we are, then we'd love to receive your feedback!

SINOIST
BOOKS

www.sinoistbooks.com *@sinoistbooks*